YOU CAN'T HIDE

EMILY SHINER

D1471862

INKUBATOR
BOOKS

Published by Inkubator Books
www.inkubatorbooks.com

ISBN (eBook): 978-1-83756-085-1
ISBN (Paperback): 978-1-83756-086-8
ISBN (Hardback): 978-1-83756-087-5

1

LIZZY

The sun beats down on my head as I pop my hip out to the side and throw my thumb into the air, jabbing it over my shoulder in a movement that hopefully screams *help me hitch a ride but don't kill me*. Even though all I want is to down a tall glass of ice water, I keep a smile on my face and wait until the last possible second of a car approaching to wipe the sheen off my forehead.

Someone has to stop. Eventually. Farther down the road, in the direction I've come from, I see the hulking mass of my car hunched over the edge of the road, as much on it as not. Each car approaching me from that direction has to slow down and move out of the way to avoid clipping it. Not that it would matter to me if they did — what's one more dent when the entire thing is destined for the scrapyard?

The vehicle approaching me is a truck with dust all over the sides and mud splashed up on its fender. Too late, I drop my hand by my side and turn, dipping my chin down to my chest and walking in the direction of town. You can tell a lot about people from the type of car they drive, and it's not that

I have anything against men in trucks, exactly, it's just that I have enough experience to know they don't always turn out to be the best humans on the planet.

Anyone willing to drive a gas guzzler at the expense of the environment likely isn't going to stop for someone like me walking along the side of the road anyway, so I'm more than a little surprised when I hear the truck approach, slow down, then idle next to me.

"You need a ride, darlin'?" The voice is loud, easy on the ears.

For a moment I resist turning to look to see who called to me, but I finally do.

He's cute. That's not the most important thing when getting rescued from the side of the highway, but it sure doesn't hurt. I need more than cute, though. I need someone with enough money to make all of my problems just disappear. I'll accept whatever help I can get with my car, but if they want to offer more, I sure won't turn them down.

"I'm fine walking," I say, but my feet make their way to the passenger-side door of the truck before I can stop them. Holding one hand over my eyes to shield them from the sun, I look in the cab, taking in how neat and clean it is. The man driving it isn't dressed in cowboy boots and dirty jeans, which is what I would have expected on a side road in Alabama, but a suit, his tie loosened at his neck, an easy grin on his face as he looks at me.

"I have no doubt you can handle yourself, but it's a bit of a haul to town, and that sun is right overhead."

He doesn't have to tell me that. I feel like I'm going to melt into a puddle if I don't get in some shade, and quick. I had a bottle of water in the car with me when it broke down, but I stupidly poured it in the radiator to see if I could get it up and running again.

It didn't work, and now my mouth is dry.

"What's your name?"

"Zachary." He flashes me a grin. Straight, white teeth. Someone's parents paid for braces. "Yours?"

"Lizzy." I pause, thinking. "Are you from here or just passing through?"

"Newly transplanted. I had to borrow a truck because I wanted to get new tires on my Lexus. I'm the new doctor in town."

A doctor? He *looks* like a doctor, happy and full of life, like he knows he has a direct line to God's ear and isn't afraid to use it if it gets him the results he wants with his patients. I like him, instantly and wholeheartedly, and I find myself opening the door before I know what I'm doing.

"If you don't mind, I just really need to get to my shift, or I'm going to be fired." As I slide into the cab of the truck, I'm struck by how different we look. He looks ... well, like the man just waltzed off the cover of *GQ*, and I'm dressed in my work uniform. A small pink half apron hangs almost down to my knees. The shoes I tugged on this morning were white, but now they have a brown tint to them from walking so far. I'm grateful not to have a mirror because I'm sure there are huge sweat stains on my white shirt, and I really don't want to have to face how I look.

"Tell me where to take you." He pulls away from the side of the road, rolls up my window, and cranks the AC to high all at the same time.

I buckle and adjust the vent so it's blowing right in my face. I feel like a dog with my head out the window, but I don't care, not when I'm no longer suffering on the side of the road.

"Do you know Pop's Diner?" Everyone in town knows Pop's. It's on the corner of the busiest intersection in town, but this guy is new, so he might not have found his way around town yet. I remember there being chatter about us getting a new doctor, someone *really good*, so good we don't deserve him. There were customers in the diner a week or so ago talking about him and wondering why he'd come here.

Why, when he could easily write his ticket for anywhere in the US, would he come to the middle of Turkey Pen, Alabama? We're lucky he's someone who doesn't hate the heat and backwards ways of Alabama, but I can't remember how long he's been around, and I never really heard why he decided to come here, of all places.

"The place with the bright blue sign out front?"

I nod, watching him drive. He has his hand draped over the wheel, the other on his thigh, his fingers tapping out a rhythm only he can hear. He's addictive to watch, and I have to stop myself from staring at him.

"I have a shift there in just a few minutes." Glancing at the time on the clock, I feel my stomach shift. Actually, my shift was a few minutes ago, but it's not like I'm going to ask the man to speed. At any rate, I'll get there when I get there, and hopefully my shift supervisor, Charlene, won't be too upset about me showing up a bit late.

"I'll get you there but on one condition."

Here it is. Men always have an ulterior motive for everything they do. I learned this a long time ago, when I was a little girl, and the lesson was so strong, so intense, that it's not something I've ever forgotten. Even without this guy telling me what he wants from me, I feel like I'm going to be sick.

I roll down the window. Town approaches quickly through the windshield, but not fast enough.

"Don't tell me you want to take me on a date." Keeping my face turned away from him, I close my eyes as the wind blows about the truck's cab. I know what men really mean when they say they want to take you on a date, and you know what? I'm not interested. I just want to be happy, and it's hard to be happy when you owe someone all the time.

He barks out a laugh.

Surprised, I turn to look at him.

"I wouldn't say no to a date with you, Lizzy, but that's not it. I'm actually a bit of a car guy and wanted to know if I could have your key to see if I could figure out what was going on with yours. I can't promise I'll be able to fix it, of course, but I'd love to take a look around. If nothing else, I'll get it towed to the garage for you. AAA is a lifesaver, don't you agree?"

I don't know, I don't have AAA. Still, there's something sincere about what he's saying and the way he glances at me before putting his eyes back on the road.

"You're a car guy?"

He nods.

"And a doctor?"

"Guilty." There's that grin again, one that could make even the most stubborn women agree to do something stupid, like hand him the keys to her broken-down vehicle without really knowing anything about him.

"And you're not married or engaged or anything? I'm not in the mood to get Margie back only to have someone take a golf club to it."

"Margie?"

"My car. And you didn't answer the question."

"No worries, I'm single." As if to prove his point, he holds up his left hand and wiggles his finger at me. No ring, no tan line. But that doesn't really prove anything, does it? My mind starts to race as I think about all the ways he could be lying to me, but then I take a deep breath.

No. I'm not going down that path. Sometimes people are just nice. Sometimes they really don't want anything from you. And even if I find out later that this guy isn't nice and does, in fact, want something from me, what does it matter? I can handle myself. I can easily take care of anything that comes my way.

"Okay. You can have my key. My shift ends at ten." Shifting my weight forward, I dig in my pocket and pull out my car key, handing it over to him before I can change my mind or, as my dad used to say, *have an attack of brains.* As soon as his voice echoes in my head, I push it out again.

I'm not going to think about my father.

"I'll see you at ten." He slows the truck, putting it in park, and I'm honestly surprised to see that we're at Pop's. The time with him flew by, and I unbuckle, grabbing the handle and preparing to jump out as quickly as possible.

But he stops me.

His hand is on my arm. I stiffen.

"Lizzy, I'll either have your car up and running by the time you get off shift, or I'll be here to drive you home. Don't you worry about a thing, okay?" When I don't immediately respond, he takes his hand off my arm and places it back on the steering wheel.

There. I can think better when he's not touching me. I put a smile on my face and turn to him. "Thank you. I would never have made it here without you stopping to pick me up."

"It was the right thing to do." He holds my gaze for a beat longer than necessary. "Have a good shift, Lizzy. I'll see you soon."

Then I'm out of the car, my feet planted on the dirty parking lot. I slam the door shut and hear him drive away before finally allowing myself to turn and look at him. He doesn't look back, and I can't tell if that makes me happy or sad.

He's a nice guy, that's all. A nice guy doing a nice thing for a stranger who was in a lot of trouble. I'll see him at ten when he tells me my car is a lost cause, and then I probably won't ever see him again. And honestly? That's fine. I don't need someone like that in my life, don't need the complication of dating someone.

And I especially don't need someone digging into my past.

2

BETH

I f I make it to my husband's cabin without falling in a snowbank or dying of cold, I will kill him for dragging me through these woods.

I knew, deep in my heart, when he suggested this trip, that I should have stayed home. It's not like we're seeing friends and family, not like we're going to have fun for the next week, but the thought of poor Ian cleaning out his family's old cabin to put it on the market to pay for IVF spurred me into a moment of weakness, and I agreed to help him.

And now I regret it.

Leaning forward against the wind, I shift my backpack a bit higher, exhaling hard as I do. It wouldn't be a difficult hike through these dark woods if it weren't for the snow. Ian's cutting a path through it, his legs slicing the thick drifts so I can have an easier time, but it still cakes on my boots, dragging me down. I feel like my feet are dipped in concrete and I'm about to be thrown into the river for wronging the mob.

"At least then this would be over soon." I mutter the words to myself, completely unaware that Ian is listening.

"What?" He stops, turning. As soon as he slows down, the wind buffets us even more.

I plant my feet in the slippery snow and look up at him, trying to look innocent.

"Did you say something?"

"Must have been the wind." I hate lying to my husband, but there's no way I'm going to tell him the truth about how my feet feel like ice cubes, how my fingers are going to be permanently frostbitten, how I want nothing more than to be anywhere but here. I'm prepared for North Carolina winters, where the snow stays for a day or two before melting. It doesn't even really have time to get dirty along the side of the road before it disappears, and I'm able to check the mail without looking like I'm headed out on an Arctic expedition.

But this isn't North Carolina. It's New York. *Upper* New York, to be precise, about as close to Canada as you can get without making a run for the border and enjoying poutine for lunch. Here, instead of my favorite Blue Ridge Mountains, I'm surrounded not only by towering, jagged Adirondacks, but also by lakes, huge bodies of water that make the wind even colder as it sweeps across their glasslike surfaces. I want to be home, in my pajamas, holding a mug of tea. I want to be reading a book, maybe taking a long bath, definitely not trudging through snow in tight snow boots Ian insisted I buy new for the trip.

There's a blister on my right heel. I feel it rubbing. Adjusting my gait isn't helping.

He turns back and points. I have to squint to see what he's trying to show me. Thick branches block our path, all of them bent with a heavy layer of snow. We'll brush through them in a moment, knocking the snow to the ground, leaving some trace that we were here. Right now it's easy to believe we're the only ones out here for miles and miles.

The last time we saw any sign of another living person

was when we filled up the rental at the gas station. It was a Prius, of all things, the most ridiculous car to drive anywhere north of the Mason-Dixon Line, and it was pretty clear both the attendant and I had the same impression of how much farther the car was going to go in this storm. He had leered at us when Ian asked him if the roads up in this direction had been cleared. The man was laughing at our choice of vehicle, but Ian didn't care.

My husband has been laser-focused on getting to the cabin from the moment he had the idea of coming up here to clean it out so we can put it on the market. Honestly, I'm just glad we made it as far as we did, all the way to the gravel lot where Ian and his family would park their cars before commencing the short walk through the woods to the cabin.

Not that it feels short right now. I feel like we've been walking for miles even though I probably take longer strolls checking out all the fresh produce at Food City.

"I don't see anything." I'm still peering into the woods, doing my best to please my husband by catching sight of what he's trying to show me, but I swear I can't see a thing. It all looks the same out here, swirling white and dark branches, a sky that feels like it's hanging so low it seems to be pressing down on the two of us.

"The cabin. It's right through these woods." He sounds happy, and I force a smile.

Great. The cabin. The one place I don't want to be right now, and the only shelter around here for miles, unless I want to fight my way back to the Prius and then pray the roads have suddenly been plowed. Apparently, we're right off a main road, so the plow should be here relatively quickly, but I don't want to take my chances.

Turning, I look at the path we've already made. It's mostly gone. I can see dips and valleys in the snow where our prints were, but the snow is pouring from the sky now; a heavy blanket of it that coats my eyelashes and covers up any sign that we were here. We haven't been walking that long, yet there's no way I'd ever find my way back without Ian.

Turning back, I'm surprised to see my husband forging on ahead without me. He must think I'm right on his tail. That, or he's so excited to finally be back at the cabin after all these years that he's not thinking about anything but himself.

I start after him.

I don't have a choice.

One foot in front of the other.

"Beth!" His voice carries back to me, more of a shadow of a sound than anything else. "You've got to see this! Hurry up!"

3

LIZZY

By the time ten o'clock rolls around, I feel dead on my feet and ready to drive home, count my tips, and pass out. Instead, the realization hits me that I don't have a car, that I'm completely dependent on the kindness of a stranger, and I stagger to my feet in the back room, where I was talking with Jenny and Charlene.

"You okay there, Lizzy?" Charlene was angry at me for showing up late to my shift, but Jenny was thrilled to get a few extra tables and the tips they brought with them. Now, though, my boss is over that anger and back in the role of a loving mother figure. "You look a little upset about something."

"I forgot that my car broke down," I tell them. The restaurant had been packed, all the tables full, and this is the first time the three of us have had a chance to sit down and talk since I showed up. "I don't know how I'll get home."

"I can drive you." Jenny stands, stretching. "You don't live too far out, do you?"

I do. I live on the outskirts of town, far away from what counts as civilization here in Turkey Pen, and I really don't want anyone from work feeling like they have to drive me all the way out there.

"I'll be fine," I say, beating her to the door and looking out into the restaurant. We've put all the chairs up on the tables, the lights are off, and the whole place looks a bit spooky. Outside, though, the parking lot is well lit. The owner, Jerry, did that after someone was killed in the parking lot last year. He said he'd rather pay for the lights and electricity than walk up on that scene ever again.

"It's not a problem." Jenny grabs her purse, slinging it over her chest like a bandolier. "Let's go."

Before she can push past me, I see someone walk up to the door. He presses his hands against it, then knocks on the glass. The three of us freeze before I remember Zachary.

He promised he'd be here. Did he mean it?

"That's my ride," I announce, giving the two women smiles. "I'll see you girls Monday. Have a good day off tomorrow." According to Jerry, Sunday is the Lord's day. Much like Chick-fil-A does, he believes in resting on Sunday. It's a bit of a joke among those of us who work here, but I have to admit it's nice to sleep in.

Hurrying through the restaurant, I unlock the front door and slip out. Almost immediately, the bolt clicks into place behind me, but I don't look to see whether Jenny or Charlene was the one to lock me out. I'm sure they're sizing Zachary up, and I have no doubt my phone will blow up later as they reach out to discuss him.

"You showed up."

He frowns. "Of course I did. Did you really think I was going to leave you hanging when you were so clearly needing help? No, that's not how I operate." He holds out my key, letting it dangle from his fingers. "Your chariot awaits."

"You fixed it?" Grabbing the key, I squeal a little. "Oh my gosh, how did you do that? There's no way the garage was going to be able to take care of it that quickly, not on a weekend. I know Glover works miracles over there, but he likes to take it easy on the weekends."

"I called in a professional favor." Zachary looks pleased at how happy I am to have my car back.

"You and your favors. I guess it worked out okay in the end, didn't it?" I slip my key into my pocket. Behind him I see Margie, a beat-up Civic with brakes that need replacing, looking completely out of place next to his Lexus.

So he wasn't lying about the truck not being his. Still, as much as I appreciate what he's done for me, it's time for me to get home. Meeting Zachary was a nice distraction from the rest of the day, but that's all it was. A distraction. I don't need to try to date someone, and I sincerely doubt a man like him would be interested in someone like me.

"It worked out perfectly." He turns, looking at our two cars. "I got to tinker a little on Margie and then called in backup when things weren't going the way I wanted them to."

"Well, thank you." My feet are screaming at me to get home, take off my sneakers, and rest them on the coffee table. I'm exhausted, probably smell, and really just want to get to sleep.

"Let me take you to dinner tomorrow." He steps to the side, making it clear I can walk past him at any moment, but his eyes are locked on my face. "Please, Lizzy. I know we don't really know each other, but I enjoyed having you in the truck and getting to talk to you a little bit. Let's talk more."

I hesitate. Momma always said that when a nice man asks you to dinner, you should thank them and go, if just for the free food more than anything else. She said a lot of things, some of which I don't agree with, but some of which I do. And I never turn down free food.

"I'll go to dinner with you," I announce, surprising both

of us. "But you're not picking me up. I'll meet you there. Blister Pizza, six pm. How does that sound?"

"Sounds wonderful, like a date." Looking over my head, he waves at Jenny and Charlene, who I now see are watching me through the front window of the restaurant. Yep, I'm going to be fielding a lot of interested texts later.

"I'll see you then." Before I can stand there and be even more awkward, I take my leave, practically running for Margie. She fires up without a complaint, the first time she's done that in years, and I hurry home, leaving Zachary in the parking lot. The entire drive home I keep looking in my rearview mirror, half-imagining I see his headlights behind me.

But there's nothing. He's not back there; he's not following me. Not all men are the same, and maybe he's one of the good ones.

Still, as soon as I get in my little apartment and lock the front door, I open my laptop. It's an old Dell I bought second-hand when I moved to Alabama, and while it still works, it's definitely in need of hospice care. It takes a moment to fire up; then I'm searching his name.

There he is. Dr. Zachary Pierce. Board-certified family practice doctor. He went to medical school at Duke University and completed his residency at the McGaw Medical Center in Chicago. Even though he's young, it looks like he has a great reputation.

So what in the world would bring a man like him to Turkey Pen, Alabama? I guess that's a question I need to ask him, because after half an hour of more searching, including for his social media and any newspaper mentions of him, I have no idea what would bring him down here.

Maybe he wants to be a big fish in a small pond. Some people are like that. They get their kicks from making sure they're the most important person around, but I didn't get that impression from him. Still, there has to be a good reason he moved here.

The only people living in Turkey Pen are those unfortunate enough to have been born here and then not been able to escape, like Charlene and Jerry, and people like me who run to a small town to hide.

Everyone says you can hide in a big city, like New York City, but I don't think that's true. When you want to make sure nobody is going to find you, then you need to huddle down in a place people aren't likely to look.

Like Turkey Pen, Alabama.

Hey, it's worked for me.

4

BETH

I push out of the woods, one last branch snagging on my jacket. There's a soft sound as it rips through the fabric, and I swear, hoping Ian won't notice the tear when we're finally inside. He's standing right in front of me, his bulk blocking my view of what has him so excited, so I step to the side, grabbing his arm for support as I break away from the path he's made in the snow. My hands are warm from being gloved and shoved in the pockets of my coat, and I'm surprised at how quickly I feel the cold cutting through the wool.

"What in the world?" The words leave my lips as I finally register what he found. Ahead of us is the cabin, a smaller building than I was expecting, but I'm not looking at the cracked window, the sagging front porch, the way the roof definitely looks like it's going to collapse under the weight of the snow. My eyes flick over all these things before landing on what's in front of us on the ground, and I exhale hard, taking a step back, pulling on Ian as I do. "We should go."

"We're not going. It probably just got cold and lost and died here." He takes a step, and even though I want to hang onto him for support and safety, I let him go. My hand slips from his arm, but he barely notices, he's so focused on the deer in front of him.

It couldn't have been here very long, not with how strong this storm is. There's a light layer of snow on it, the white flakes masking some of the dark brown fur. Ian brushes snow away from the deer's head, and the glassy eye stares up into the sky, unblinking, even with icy bits landing on it.

I wince.

Anyone who has ever seen a horror movie or read a book scary enough to make them worry about whether or not all the doors of their house are locked knows that finding a dead animal where you don't expect one is a bad sign. Ian must not have the same sense of self-preservation I do. He's leaning over the animal now, clearing it of snow, looking for ... something.

"What are you doing? Let's get inside and just warm up if you don't want to turn back." I stamp my feet to drive my point home and glance up at the cabin. The jagged glass in the window looks ominous, but surely I'd be happier in there, right? Safer.

"I think it was shot." He presses down on the animal's side, and when I look closer, I see red. "See? A hunter probably hit it, and it ran. The snow is so thick you can't really track easily, and it just died here. I bet it hasn't been dead for very long."

"Just leave it." There's a whine in my voice I don't like and don't recognize, and Ian doesn't look at me. "Seriously, Ian, what are we going to do with that?"

"We can't waste it." He stands, brushing his hands together. "You can't just waste a life like that, Beth." There's a flash of sadness on his face, but it disappears just as quickly.

"Okay, but we didn't kill it. We're not wasting it. Someone else is." I'm suddenly desperate to get inside the cabin even though it's obvious it's not going to offer a lot of protection from the storm. Glancing back up, I eyeball the chimney. Is it still functional? I think I see a curl of smoke rise from it, but shake my head.

The snow is thick, the wind strong. Whatever I think I'm seeing is just an illusion in this terrible storm. Wishful thinking as I imagine what it will be like to warm myself in the cabin.

"What about heat?" I have to raise my voice to make sure he can hear me over the wind.

"My parents had electricity run out here before they died. Cost a fortune, but as long as the lines weren't knocked out, you'll be able to see what you're doing as soon as you get in there. The lights should come right on, but plan to start a fire just in case."

Just in case. Love that. I don't immediately respond.

"How about this? You head into the cabin and see if you can start a fire. I'll clean this guy really quick, or at least do my best. There's no reason why we can't enjoy the meat when the hunter is probably already back at home warming up."

"But what if he's not?" The thought of someone like the gas station attendant coming to our cabin looking for his deer worries me. "He might show up at any time and then be mad that you took his deer. Besides, I never heard a gunshot. It's just weird."

"Sound travels differently in snow like this. It's decided, Beth. Do you have a lighter?"

I nod. Of course I have a lighter. Ian stuffed my backpack with everything I'd need on this trip. But I'm still not convinced.

He sees the expression on my face and sighs. "Doesn't some venison sound good for dinner? You can fry it up, add some pasta from my pack; we'll have a great little meal. Trust me, Beth, you'll love it."

My stomach rumbles at the thought. I hope we packed enough food for this trip, but I'm not really sure. Most of what we bought is still in the back of the Prius since the two of us didn't stand a chance at carrying it through the woods. So maybe Ian's right, as much as I hate to admit it. It's shameful to waste a life like this, and just because I wasn't brought up hunting to put food on the table in the winter doesn't mean he wasn't. He's told me before about going out into the woods with his dad when he was hungry, and this is just an extension of that.

If he can really take care of the deer out in the snow, then I can go in the cabin and start a fire. It's not like I've ever skinned a deer before, and I'm not interested in learning how to right now, when it's freezing out and getting darker by the minute.

"Okay. I'll warm it up in there," I say, forcing a smile to my lips. It feels fake, a mask, but I don't think Ian notices. "By the time you're done, it will feel like a five-star hotel."

"Great." He sounds cheered now that I'm willing to go along with his plan. "That's great, Beth. Before you go, though, I need your help moving this guy to the back shelter."

He can't be serious. I stare at my husband, who's already shrugging out of his pack and putting it on the porch stairs. When he reaches out for mine, I slip it from my shoulders without thinking. Immediately I'm even colder than I was a moment ago, and I rub my hands up and down my arms. This storm is no joke, but since this was the only week we both had off work, we didn't really have any other time to come here.

It was now or never. Just like moving the deer.

I don't want to do it, so I turn my head to the side so I don't have to look at the deer's fur as I squat down and grab the back legs. They're thinner than I would have thought, and

I say a little prayer of thanks I can't feel the coarse fur through my gloves. When I open my eyes and look up, Ian is staring at me.

"Ready? Lift with your legs. Just watch your step, okay? I don't want you to trip, Beth."

The thought of landing face-first on a dead deer is more than enough to help me stay on my feet. I try not to think about what we're doing as I carry the animal with my husband to the back shed. It looks like more of a lean-to than anything else, barely blocking the snow, but Ian looks thrilled when we put the animal on the rickety wooden table.

"I'm going inside," I say, desperate to get out of the storm, away from the deer, away from what Ian is about to do. He gives me a small nod as I wipe my hands on my jeans. "Don't freeze to death."

Ian says something in response, but the wind whips it away before I can make out the words. I should look back, should try to figure out what it was he just said, but instead I hunker down farther into my coat, shoulder into the wind, and hurry towards the cabin, grabbing our packs before I head up the stairs. The doorknob turns easily under my touch, and I step through, waving my hand in front of my face to knock down any spiderwebs.

There aren't any.

But that's not the biggest shock.

5

LIZZY

It's been three months since I met Zachary Pierce, MD, and even though I did my best to keep my walls up in case he's not who he says he is, I can't find any proof that he's not telling me the truth. He's perfect, or as close to perfect as a man can possibly be, and even though I told myself I'd never get married or fall in love, I feel like I'm on that slippery slope towards wanting the house with the white picket fence and the 2.5 kids. Maybe a golden retriever, too. A garden. Some window boxes I can water every morning after making the entire family blueberry pancakes for breakfast.

I'm so wrapped up in my fantasy of the future that I don't realize Zachary is staring at me, obviously waiting for an answer to some question I definitely didn't hear, until he clears his throat. That sound, combined with his raised eyebrows and the hopeful expression on his face, snaps me back to reality.

"I don't want to admit this to you," I begin, but he cuts me off.

"But you weren't listening. Don't worry, Lizzy, I could tell by the expression on your face you were somewhere else right now."

"Not true." Leaning forward, I grab his hands and give them a squeeze. The remains of our dinner are on the table, some delicious salmon he whipped up and glasses of wine. There's one more swallow in mine, but I ignore it, keeping my eyes locked on the man across from me. "I was thinking about our future and what I thought it was going to look like."

"Me too." He flushes, a cute habit I don't think I'll ever tire of. "So let me ask you again. Will you marry me?"

My mind works overtime as he lets go of one of my hands, reaching into his pocket before holding a ring out in front of me. I gasp, and then he's on his knees next to me, slipping the ring on my finger before I even have a chance to answer. It happens so quickly that I don't have time to think things through, let alone form any words, but really, what would I say?

No? It's laughable to think about turning this man down. It's a joke that I would ever say no to him, not to the most perfect man I've ever met in my life.

"Marry me, Lizzy. You're perfect for me."

He doesn't say *I love you*, but he's said it so many other times in the past that I don't hold it against him. I'm perfect for him, which is something I've never been for anyone in my entire life.

"Yes," I squeal; then he's up, pulling me to my feet, wrapping his arms around me and kissing me. There are tears on my face, and he wipes them away, pulling me by the hand away from the table. I think for sure he's leading me to the bedroom to celebrate, but instead of turning down the hall, he leads me to the front door, throwing it open and gesturing for me to follow him onto the porch.

I do. But I'm confused.

A new Lexus sits in the driveway, a huge red bow on top of it. It's white, while his is black, but other than that, they're the same car.

"Where's Margie?" The question is out of my mouth before I know what I'm saying. His expression changes, so fleeting I barely see it, but then he smiles again.

"You needed a better car. I knew you would say yes, Lizzy, and I wanted to make sure you wouldn't just be safe driving around town, but that you would look good as my wife. The last thing I needed was my wife driving the junker around."

"Oh, thank you." I say the words, but inside I'm confused, the emotion I'm feeling battling against the joy I felt a moment ago. I loved Margie, and he'd fixed her up for me. No, she wasn't the nicest car in Turkey Pen, but she got me from point A to point B, and now that I moved in with him and quit my job at Pop's, it wasn't like I really went a lot of places. Mostly to the store or to the park or to visit him at work. She worked just fine for what I needed.

"You don't sound happy." He turns, taking me by the shoulders. His grip is tight, but I chalk it up to him just being excited and worried that I'm not matching his energy.

So I turn on the charm. "It's amazing, Zachary, thank you." Throwing my arms around him, I give him a big kiss. "Seriously, it's probably the nicest thing anyone has ever done for me before."

"Well, I am going to be your husband." There's a note of pride in his voice, and I can't help the way it warms me from the inside. He wants to be my husband. He really loves me. It's a strange feeling, one I've never really felt before, and I don't want to let it go.

But he steps back, his gaze suddenly critical. "I have a photographer set up for tomorrow for the two of us to get our engagement photos taken. I want to be able to send out announcements and put one in the paper."

"Oh, is that a thing people do?" It strikes me as odd that he'd have the photographer and the new car lined up before even proposing to me, but that just tells me how confident he was that I wasn't going to turn him down. I should be grateful that he feels that confident about our relationship and how strong it is.

"Oh, sure. And I want everyone to know I'm off the market." He kisses me again, then opens the door for me to follow him back into the house.

I notice he doesn't say that he wants everyone to know I'm off the market, but I guess an ex-waitress is a lot different than a doctor. He's a public figure, so well-known that it's pretty much impossible for the two of us to go anywhere without someone recognizing him.

Out to a nice dinner? A grateful patient is likely to send over a bottle of wine.

Checking out at the grocery store? Someone will probably stop him to thank him for treating them.

It was a little strange to me at first, especially when I'm so used to doing everything I possibly can to blend into the background, but Zachary takes it all in stride and wants me to do the same. So I do. I smile at his patients, meet the doctors he works with, and never question anyone who wants a bit of his time.

After all, I'm the one he comes home to at night, and now I'm the one wearing a giant rock on my finger.

Looking down at it, part of me wishes I could show my parents. They wouldn't be able to believe that someone like Zachary would really want to marry me. I can just hear the surprise in their voices if they were to see this rock. I'd love to rub it in.

If they were alive.

"First thing tomorrow I want you to go shopping." Zachary takes my hands and gently pulls me so I sit next to him on the sofa. The leather still needs to be broken in. It's a bit uncomfortable to sit on for long periods of time, but I know he loves the way it looks. He loves how expensive everything in our home is.

"Oh, for the photos? You don't think I have a dress I can wear?"

A small smile, one that looks like more a smirk and then changes, spreads so it takes up his entire face. "Oh, Lizzy, you have no idea what I've done for you. Go look in your closet."

I do, almost stumbling over my feet in an effort to get to the room we share together. Moving in with Zachary was a huge step, but it didn't feel big at the time. It's insane, how quickly the two of us have moved and how fast our relationship has progressed, but every step has felt just right.

Taking a deep breath, I grab the double doors that will open the closet. It's probably silly to want to take my time so I can really enjoy whatever it is he has in there for me, but I don't want to rush through this. I have no idea what surprise he has for me, but I was out grocery shopping and then at the tanning salon for a while this morning, so he had plenty of time to pull something off.

Will it be full of new dresses he bought me? I can just picture them nestled in between some of my old favorites, the dresses that fit like a second skin and comfort me as soon as I pull them on. I may not have kept a lot of things from my time before moving to Alabama, but there are some pieces of clothing that sing to me. They make me feel like I'm truly the person I'm meant to be when I pull them on.

Some people would say that sounds crazy, but I say those people have never worn the right dress.

"Open it." Zachary's behind me, the excitement in his voice palpable.

I take another deep breath, then throw the doors open. Overhead, the automatic light clicks on.

I blink.

There's nothing.

"Where are my clothes?" Swallowing hard, I try to keep the tears out of my voice. Everything I had in here when I left this morning, all of my jeans and tops I chose myself, the dresses I love, the shoes that still fit after years of having them, everything is gone. The shelves, made from mahogany and polished to shine, sit empty.

Velvet hangers clatter when I run my hand down them.

"My clothes are gone." Even to my ears my voice is flat. "What did you do with my clothes?" I turn to look at Zachary, fully expecting him to look repentant. I'm sure there's going to be a question on his face, him wondering if I forgive him, him wondering if he messed up.

Instead, he tilts his chin up, stares me in the eyes. The only expression on his face is pleasure, and the way he stares at me makes my stomach twist.

"I got rid of all of your clothes, Lizzy. You're going to be my wife, and you need to look the part. You've been tanning like I told you to, yes?"

I nod, mute. My mind is screaming at me not to answer him, but I can't help the fact that I love this man. I want to respond to him, want to make him happy.

"You're so good." He murmurs the words, reaches out, lightly touches my chin.

I pull back. My heart hammers out an uneven rhythm, and I have one terrible thought that at least, if I were to have a heart attack or a stroke caused by the stress of what this man just did, he's a doctor and could help me.

He'd save me.

"I can be your wife and still wear the clothes I like."

Now he laughs, and the sound is so at odds with the expression on his face that I take an involuntary step back from him.

"No, Lizzy, you can't. You need to look the part, need to make sure you don't embarrass me."

"I wouldn't. Why would you say that?" Tears sting my eyes now, and I blink them away, angrily reaching up with one hand to wipe the one tear that escapes my blinking and works its way down my cheek. "You love me the way I am. You told me I'm different, I'm special." My voice breaks. I'm going to replay this moment in my head over and over and hate the fact that my voice breaks, I just know it.

"Lizzy," he murmurs my name. Reaches for me.

I step back.

"Don't be silly, Lizzy. Of course I love you. I love the person you're going to be, too. You'll go shopping tomorrow; you'll have a great time. Then, for our photos, you'll be perfect. You'll marry me, and we'll be happy. I promise."

"I don't want this." Even though I haven't given any thought to what I'm saying or doing, I twist the ring on my finger. It pops off, and I hold it out to him. "We need to talk about this. We're not on the same page."

He doesn't reach to take it. "Put it back on. You're my fiancée now."

"No." The diamond catches the light and throws it, sparkling brighter than any stone I've ever seen before. "You can't just expect me to change myself like that for you."

"I can. And I do. Put the ring back on, Lizzy."

I can barely see him through my tears. Just a few minutes before, I'd been desperate to make sure he didn't see me crying, but now it doesn't matter. I just want to get away from him. I need time to think. To clear my head.

"I'm going out," I say. "Give me the keys to my car." Not *my* car, not Margie, but the car he bought for me. It seemed like such a lovely gift just a few minutes ago.

"If you walk out of this room, Lizzy, I promise you

everyone in town will know what you did before you moved to Alabama. Is that what you want?"

I freeze. Take a beat. Try to wrap my mind around the words ringing in my ears. "What did you just say?"

He's grinning now, showing all of his perfectly white, perfectly straight teeth. Everything about this man is perfect, from his head to his toes, and he wants me to be, too. Maybe that's not too much to ask. Maybe I should just shut up and do what he wants.

But now he has me really concerned.

"I said, Lizzy, that if you don't want everyone to know what you did before you fled Louisiana and ended up here, then you need to put that ring back on your finger. Put a smile on your face. Let the entire world know how happy you are to be engaged to me, or I'll let the entire world know the truth about who you really are."

6

BETH

A cat greets me, meowing as it rubs against my legs, the bell on its red collar tinkling loudly.

"Hey there, bud," I say, dropping the backpacks before bending down to scratch it under its chin. The cat pulls back, and I yank off a glove, letting it sniff my fingers before trying again. This time, my fingers sink into its soft fur, and it begins to let out a loud purr. "What's your name? Huh?" Carefully I turn the tag on the collar so I can get a better look at it, pulling my phone from my pocket and turning on the flashlight to be able to read it. "Mya, huh? Well, Mya, what are you doing in here?"

If I'm to believe Ian, this cabin has been deserted for years. So how in the world is there a cat with a collar on hanging out inside? There's a cracked window, sure, but that wouldn't give the cat nearly enough room to squeeze through, and besides, the nearest place must be ... well, I'm not entirely sure. Ian has told me that it's not uncommon for people here to travel by snowmobile in the winter, and also not uncommon to go a long time without seeing your neighbor.

So where did this cat come from?

Standing, I watch as Mya winds around my legs, and I reach for the light switch, my fingers fumbling against the wall until I find it. The light clicks on, the sound loud in the silence, and I jump before letting out a low laugh and turning off the flashlight on my phone.

Silly of me to think anything else would happen besides the light turning on. Silly of me to get all worked up over ... what? Walking into an empty cabin with my husband right outside? Besides, the cabin isn't really empty, not with Mya here to greet me. Still, I'm nervous, and I turn and look out into the growing dark, shielding my eyes from the overhead light with one hand as I search for where Ian's working on dressing the deer.

Nothing. I can't see more than a few feet into the swirling mass of white right outside the door. Even the porch, which is covered, is quickly turning white as snow builds up on it. I kick my feet against the doorframe before slipping off my boots. The release of pressure on my heel feels amazing, and I sigh, then lean the boots up against the house. Ian would be ticked to see puddles on the floor in here if I brought them in and the snow melted off them.

Tugging the door shut, I yank on it until the latch clicks. It's hard to lock in place, which must explain why the door was so easy to open a moment ago. Ian probably didn't pull it all the way shut the last time he was here. That's a better alternative for me to believe than the thought that someone else was in here.

But it would explain how Mya got in here.

That thought lingers for a moment before I push it away.

Now, finally, I get to pay attention to the cabin. I'd caught a glimpse of the room when I turned on the light, but now is my first chance to really look at it. The cabin looks tiny from the outside, and from all of the stories Ian told me, I already knew it wasn't going to be spacious. Still, I had no idea how small it would really be.

I'm standing in an open room with Mya twining around my ankles. In front of me is a small table with a single chair pulled out. A closed book sits on the table, and I walk over to get a better look at it. *The Art of Never Letting Go.* I've never heard of the author, and I flip a few pages before closing the book, then run my fingers across the top of the table.

I'm fully expecting to pull my fingers away and have them covered in dust, but I'm shocked to find that the table is clean. Besides the book, there's nothing — no dust, no dead moths, nothing that I would think should be present in a house that's been locked up and in disuse for years.

Someone had to have been in this cabin.

Recently.

I want to push that thought from my mind, and I give my head a little shake to clear it.

It doesn't help.

Turning away from the table, I walk over to the kitchen. It's in a small room off the main one, and the cracked window is in here. From the outside I couldn't tell that someone had already hung plastic up to block the worst of the wind, taping it carefully on the window frame to keep out the wind. Without thinking, I reach up and lightly touch it, shocked at just how cold it is outside. Feeling the chill reminds me I'm supposed to be getting it warmed up in here so when Ian comes in from dressing the deer, he won't be too cold.

Leaving the kitchen, I walk back into the main room. From here, I can see a small bathroom as well as a bedroom, both behind partly open doors. I want to explore, want to look for more signs of someone being in here recently, but instead I grab some newspaper from the floor by the door, ready to start a roaring fire.

Mya leans on my leg, still purring, and I pat her head

before smoothing out the paper in my hand. The headline is about a young girl with cancer who walked across the state to help raise money for other kids with leukemia. I remember that happening — it even made the news down in North Carolina. Without giving it much thought, I glance at the date.

This morning.

The door, the cat, the book on the table. I stand, dropping the paper and wiping my hands on my jeans. Someone was here, someone was *living* here, and they could come back at any moment.

Or they're already here.

Watching me.

I freeze. Adrenaline is supposed to spur you into action, but right now it feels like I can't move a muscle. As much as I'd love to flee this house, to get out, to run and never look back, I can't do that. I can't seem to turn around, nor can I make myself walk to the door to try to get Ian's attention.

There's a thud from the back of the house, and I turn slowly, my eyes wide. My heart pounds in my chest, and I feel sweat break out on my brow. Fear like this makes my stomach hurt, makes me feel like I'm going to be sick. I don't know what caused the thump, what else could be in the cabin, but I have to find out if it's whoever has been squatting in here.

Or maybe I should get out of here.

"Oh, shit," I mutter. My feet hurt. My legs feel tight. It honestly feels like I just ran a marathon. Every muscle screams for me to sit back down and ignore whatever that sound was, but I can't do that. "Oh, shit, shit, shit."

Swearing is my bad habit. Ian hates it, has from the day we met. We were walking in opposite directions down the sidewalk, and I ran into him. Or he into me. His coffee went all over my shirt, my hot chocolate splashed onto his shoes, and I couldn't help the four-letter words that escaped my lips.

After he stopped scowling at my language, he began to laugh; then he asked me out.

I force myself to put one foot in front of the other. Each step takes me closer to the two doors across the room — the bathroom and the bedroom. Although I don't want to go in there by myself, stepping outside to call Ian for help doesn't seem like much of a better option. Who knows how long it would take him to get in here? The person, if that's what made the noise, could already be long gone by then.

I don't have a choice. I have to know.

Mya rubs once more against my legs, then jumps up onto the old sofa. She blinks at me and curls into a doughnut. Taking some hope from the fact that she doesn't seem worried about what I might encounter, I tiptoe to my backpack and carefully pull a knife from the side pocket.

The blade makes a soft *snick* as I flick it open. Holding it tightly, I cross the cabin to the two doors on the other side.

The bathroom door whines a little as I push it open. My hand trembles as I reach in and flick on the light, revealing a toilet, sink, and a shower. The curtain is pulled back, so I can easily see the room is empty, but I don't miss the toothpaste on the edge of the sink.

Someone wasn't just in here to stay warm in the storm.

They live here.

And if they're not in the bathroom, that means they have to be in the bedroom.

7

LIZZY

The overhead lights in the kitchen are so bright it's difficult for me to fight back the headache that has been slowly blooming here since Zachary invited our guests over. They're in the dining room now, I can hear their low voices and occasional peals of laughter, but I'm hoping and praying as I open the oven and take out the beef Wellington.

"Please be perfect," I mutter, lightly pressing my finger into the top of one of them. The dough is golden brown and looks perfectly baked, but I've been practicing making this all week, and I know how easy it is for the dough to be under-cooked, for the layer of minced mushrooms to soak into the dough and cause it all to be a soggy mess.

Yesterday I nailed it. It was perfect, the crust was golden and flaky, the beef was perfect in the middle. But yesterday doesn't matter, does it? I have to nail it today. *Right now.*

Sweating now, I wipe my hand across my forehead and plate the four Wellingtons before adding garlic mashed pota-toes and roasted carrots. Everything is perfect, I timed it all to come out of the oven at the same time, and Zachary is going to love this.

He has to.

Loading the plates onto a tray, I put a smile on my face and walk through the swinging door that leads from the kitchen into the dining room. Immediately the conversation at the table stops, and Zachary as well as Dr. and Mrs. Haversham all look up at me.

"I don't know how you do it, Lizzy," Carla says, half-rising to help me.

I notice how my husband lightly rests his hand on her arm to prevent her from helping me. Anger rises in me, hot and fast, at the fact he won't let someone who clearly wants to help me do just that, but I keep the smile on my face.

"Oh, this is nothing. I found the recipe late last night when I was still undecided about what to make for dinner and whipped it up this afternoon." The lie comes easily, and I glance at Zachary to see how happy he'll be with what I just said. His eyes are locked on mine. Waiting.

Did I sound too prideful? Before anyone can say anything in response, I amend my statement. "Of course, when you're married to someone with great taste like Zachary, you really just want to make them happy."

A shadow of a smile crosses his face.

Carla laughs and winks at her husband. "You hear that, Eric? Maybe the reason why I'm not a great cook is because you don't have great taste."

The three of them dissolve into laughter, and I put their plates down, making sure I don't accidentally knock someone's elbow. Then, before I can be asked, I grab the half-drunk bottle of wine from the sidebar and top off everyone's glasses. Except for mine. I need to make sure I've got my head about me and can handle any questions that come my way.

"It really does look wonderful, wife," Zachary murmurs, taking me by the hand before I can reach my seat.

My skin crawls, literally feeling that there are dozens of caterpillars marching in formation up and down my arm, but all I do is smile at him.

"Thank you." I hope I don't sound like a robot. "I appreciate you letting me try something new in the kitchen."

If the Havershams were to look in our trash out back, they'd see dozens of discarded Wellingtons. I can only imagine the shock on their faces if they were to find out the truth about how hard I worked on dinner tonight and how perfect it had to be.

For a moment I let my mind wander, imagining grabbing Carla by the hand. I could pull her out back to the trash, demand she lift the lid. The kitchen trash bags aren't super thick, and it would take hardly any effort to press my finger through the white plastic, to pull open a hole, to show them to her.

The Wellingtons would still hold their shape the best they could. The days have been cool, the nights cold, and I'd do my best not to get my fingernails dirty as I reached in and plucked one out, holding it over my head. It would be a real *Lion King* moment, the chance for me to exclaim that *it's a boy*, and then everyone would laugh, but really they'd be horrified, and someone would finally have an idea that the perfect facade erected by my husband and patched by me to keep the cracks from growing, from making the entire thing crash to the ground in a pile of dust and lies and yelling, was just that — a facade — and then it would be over —

"Lizzy." The good doctor Eric Haversham is staring at me, a bite of Wellington halfway to his mouth, the fork still drifting closer to his lips like he can't stop himself from eating even though it's clear he wants to say something to me. "This is a masterpiece. You've outdone yourself."

I look around the table. Everyone else is eating, and my Wellington sits in front of me, untouched. I have to push the thought of birthing the Wellingtons from their trash bag sac out of my mind and pick up my fork and knife. Cut off a bite. See the bright red meat inside, how the juices run just a little bit.

But not too much. If they run too much, then Zachary —

He's looking at me. Intense. I take the bite. Chew. Swallow. Do it again.

"What a wonderful recipe," I say, putting the talent at the feet of the person who wrote the recipe. I'm just a peon, just something to be used to create a meal so delicious, and I know it. "This one is a winner; what do you think, Zachary?"

"It's a ten." He sounds proud.

I feel my chest swell for a moment at the fact that he liked the meal so much; then I remember what happens when he does.

Zachary likes to rate his meals. He won't eat anything less than a nine, and if it falls below that, then I have to make it up to him.

"What's a ten?" Eric's had too much wine. So has his wife. They both have bright spots in their cheeks. He's getting sloppy. A piece of carrot fell in his lap, but he didn't seem to notice it. He's next to me, and I stare at it, bright orange and glazed against the white linen in his lap, then drag my eyes away from it.

"This Wellington. When we got married, Lizzy had the cute little idea of rating all of the new food she makes."

That's a lie.

"We love talking about recipes and making sure we're only eating the best."

He only wants the best. Sometimes I just want SpaghettiOs.

"It's a fun way to make sure we're on the same page about a meal and that we both love it."

My mind won't stop racing, even as I hear Zachary explain how the rating system works. Both the Havershams are charmed by him. They don't have to hear how he holds it against me when I don't meet his standards, how he'll scream and break dishes, how I ordered more plates just to have them on hand so we always have something to eat from when he ruins yet another plate because I overcooked something or didn't season it enough or just made something he didn't like.

"Well, it works. I think we'll have to start doing that." Carla laughs and reaches across the table with her fork to stab at Eric playfully. "Although I'm half-afraid you might rate everything I make a six or seven."

They both laugh uproariously, and I do too. I learned how to laugh even when I don't feel like it. I learned how to make it sound like I'm having the best time possible. It makes people comfortable.

But I still catch Zachary's eye. You wouldn't think I'd be so stupid to do that, not when we've been married almost a year, not when I know better than to try to read his mind and figure out what he's thinking, but I do it anyway.

I want to at least try to figure out what he's thinking so I know where I stand.

He's not laughing. He swallows some wine, his Adam's apple working hard, then puts the glass down, his fingers lightly dancing around the rim before picking up his fork again. I don't need him to speak to be able to read his mind.

You'd better not make something that is a six or a seven.

I promise you, you wouldn't be laughing.

8

BETH

Something is waiting for me in the bedroom.

There's no way around it. I can try to avoid going in there as long as I want, but that's not going to change the fact that whoever has been living in my husband's cabin is currently waiting for me. Ian is still outside, and fear screams at me that I need to let him know what's going on, but I'm honestly too afraid at this point to turn my back on the bedroom door.

It seems best just to get this over with.

I hate the way my hand trembles as I squeeze the knife tighter. I feel sweat breaking out on my skin, and I take a deep breath, forcing myself to slow down in an attempt to clear my head. Going into this rashly, with guns blazing, as it were, would be the stupidest thing I could possibly do.

No, I'll take my time. Standing outside the bedroom door, I ready myself. I'll kick it the rest of the way open, hopefully surprise whoever is in there waiting for me. If I'm able to do that and can turn on the light before they know I'm coming, then I'll be able to get the jump on them. Once the light is on and the door is open, then I'll have an easier time figuring out what I'm working with.

One.

Two.

Three.

I hear my high school soccer coach's voice in my head screaming at me that I need to try get to the ball, that I need to *stop standing there and do something, dammit,* and I do, throwing myself forward against my better judgment, my right hand sweeping out and up against the wall in a bid to connect with the light switch, my foot kicking the door open as my left hand clamps down on my knife in a death grip.

And I see ...

Nothing.

A bed. A dresser next to it, the top of it clear of any clutter. Two windows, one on either side of the bed, the curtains drawn as if to let in the light in the morning, but now showing nothing more than the dark of the snowy evening.

Under the bed, then.

Dropping to my knees, I exhale hard at the landing, my eyes focusing as I peer under the bed. There are a few boxes, all of them shoved to one side, but nothing more than that. Nothing other than the boxes, nobody hiding there, not even enough room for a grown man to try to squeeze under there without getting a cramp.

I'm alone.

My adrenaline drops, and I sigh, letting my arms sag by my body. As I do, there's a loud scraping sound, and I tense, immediately holding the knife out in front of me again. Something drags against the window, a loud sound, like fingernails on a chalkboard, and I turn in the direction of the window, desperate to see what it is.

It comes again, low and haunting, and it hits me. A branch. We're out here in the woods, surrounded by more trees than I could count, and of course they would rub up against the glass from time to time. Tension leaves my shoulders, and I feel cold, suddenly more worn out than I was a moment ago.

It takes me a moment to force myself to stand.

I really need to start that fire, or at least see if I was right earlier — that I did see a curl of smoke above the chimney. Turning out the light, I leave the bedroom and walk back into the living room. The newspaper is right where I left it, and I grab it, my hands shaking, then walk to the fireplace.

There's a metal poker leaning against the wall, and I grab it, ignoring the chill when my fingers close around it, and stab it into the coals.

They leap to life.

I should be happy it was so easy getting the fire going, but I step back, the poker falling from my hand.

The fire hadn't been out for long to flare up like that. Again I glance at the window, wondering where Ian is. Should I go to him? I'm alone in the cabin, at least for now, but who knows what's happening to him out there?

Mya jumps down from the sofa and twines around my legs. Stepping away from the fireplace, I trip over her, coming to a crouch on the floor to keep from falling.

"Mya, what's going on?" My voice shakes. I pet her, then, moving on autopilot, carefully place some larger pieces of wood on the fire. Hungry, the flames grow, the crackling sound chasing away any other fear I had of who might be living in the cabin.

And now it's time to find my husband. I need to make sure Ian is okay.

I started the fire, upheld my end of the bargain, but I can't pretend any longer that everything is okay.

Someone was here.

Someone might be coming back.

Hurrying to the door, I throw it open, a cold wind blasting into the small cabin. "Ian!" My voice whips away in the howl of the wind. "Ian, are you still out there?"

Nothing. The house was so cold when I came in here that I kept my coat on. It's still zipped up to my chin, and I hurriedly pull my boots on, fumbling in my backpack for a flashlight. The light comes on immediately, strong and bright. Ian changed out all the batteries in our flashlights before we left on this trip. He thinks of everything.

Except for what we're going to do if someone is living in the cabin.

I step out onto the porch and immediately regret it. It takes a moment to pull the door shut behind me and to make sure it's latched, and in that time I'm buffeted even more by the wind. It cuts through my jacket like a knife, the air colder since the sun has gone down. Turning away from the door, I aim the light out into the dark.

Snow reflects back at me, shining at me like millions of diamonds scattered on the ground. Huge flakes whip through the air, stinging my face.

"Ian! Where are you?"

Nothing. No movement, no answer. He could have gotten hurt, gotten lost. It's crazy to think he might not be able to find his way to the house from the little shelter where we took the deer, but it's easy to get turned around in a storm like this. He wouldn't be the first person to be just twenty feet from safety and not be able to find it when the weather turned nasty.

My mind races, my thoughts getting away from me as I think about what I would do if that happened to my husband. The thought of him alone, scared and cold, or hurt — I don't think I'm brave enough to search for him in this storm, but someone has to bring him home.

It's terrifying.

I've been brave before, brave enough for more than one lifetime, and now I just want to put that behind me. I want to let Ian take care of me, and I don't want to have to try to save myself, or anyone else.

"Ian!" Standing at the top of the stairs, I shine my light out into the snow. Just thinking about him getting lost between the shelter and here is enough to make me want to rush out to save him. But I can't. There's also a voice in the back of my head, telling me to slow down, telling me not to leave the safety of the house.

If my husband, who has spent countless hours up here, can't find his way back to the house, why should I think I'd be able to?

Fear freezes me in place. I'm not one usually struck by indecision, but now I can't seem to get my feet to move. I call for him again, hating how weak my voice sounds as it rings out and then is quickly swept away in the wind. Again I call his name, again and again, fear driving me to keep his name in my mouth.

Even though it's entirely possible someone else might hear me calling.

Movement to the right. I turn, my flashlight finding the spot almost immediately. Something shifts, moving closer. Bile burns the back of my mouth, but before I can try to make a decision about whether I should stay here or should make a run for the house, the thing in the snow straightens, morphing from some hideous creature into my husband.

"Ian!" Relief floods my voice. I hope he doesn't pick up on it.

"Beth, can you believe this snow?" He's laughing, *laughing*, like I wasn't just out here scared to death I was going to find him as a popsicle in the morning. His face is ruddy, his cheeks burning red with cold. He grabs the railing for support with one hand; the other hefts a piece of meat above his head.

Dinner. The mighty hunter has returned. For a moment, I see him as he probably was before I met him, before he grew up and settled down in a southern city, scooping up the first pretty girl he ran into. He looks younger out here, the snow sticking to his hat, his nose bright red, his lips chapped. There are deep laugh lines around his eyes as he squints up at me.

"I hope you're hungry."

"Ian." I remember how to move my feet, and I meet him halfway down the stairs, grabbing his hand to help him up the stairs. He offers me the meat, but I ignore his outstretched hand. "Someone was living here. They were here, Ian."

"What are you talking about?" He loops his arm around my shoulders, pulling me into him like the two of us are on a date. Maybe ice skating, maybe on a hike and about to come up on a lovely overlook. The weight of his arm is nice. His voice is free of concern. This is my husband, in his element, happy.

"Someone has been living here." I turn under his arm, wanting to get this conversation over with, *needing* to make him listen. To understand. "They were in here recently. There's a cat, and a book. Toothpaste." Words spill from my lips. This is serious.

"They're still in there?" He frowns, the happiness on his face disappearing. Instead of holding the meat over his head like a waiter at a fancy restaurant, he drops his arm to his side. "You saw Ryan?"

I shake my head. "No, but — wait, Ryan?" He's not making any sense, and I worry for a moment that he might have gotten so cold he's not thinking straight.

I clutch at his chest, my fingers icy cold and unwilling to cooperate. The most important thing right now is to make him understand. I need him to feel the gravity of what I'm telling him, that just because the person is gone *now* doesn't mean they're going to stay gone. Far from it, in fact. "Ian, someone was living here. If I found shelter in a storm like this, I wouldn't go far, would you?"

9

LIZZY

I'm washing up, carefully placing each plate in the drying rack so there isn't any chance of one of them getting chipped. I have an entire selection of plates to choose from when Zachary gets angry, but God forbid I break one. Not even a chip around the rim. Not even a crack. Nothing that might reflect poorly on the two of us.

Might reflect poorly on him.

"You did a good job, even with the crème brûlée." I didn't notice Zachary walking into the kitchen, but now he's here. His arms circle me, and he pulls me back into him, pressing his body against my back. "They were impressed with the meal from beginning to end. Of course, I'll have some notes for you tomorrow. I'll make sure the little mistakes that cropped up won't ever happen again."

What mistakes? The desire to scream the question at him is so strong I actually have to bite my tongue to keep from speaking. Asking him what I could have done better, what would have made him happier, won't really do any good. I fell into that trap when we were first married and I realized he knew so much about me.

He'd dangle impossible tasks over my head, and like an idiot, I'd try to complete them.

Wash all of the baseboards in the house with a tooth-brush. *But toothbrushes are so small.*

Have all of his laundry cleaned and pressed. *But he always had on clothing, didn't he, so I couldn't ever do it.*

Figure out what he wanted for dinner without asking and make it. *But he always changed his mind or lied or something.*

It became a dance between the two of us, but he's the only one who knew the steps. I kept tripping over my own two feet, and there wasn't anything I could do about it.

The worst part? He knew it. Now I know better than to try to fight him. I'm going with the flow, trying to keep him from exploding.

For now.

"I'm glad you enjoyed it as much as you did. And I think the Havershams had a wonderful time and enjoyed it, as well." I pause, letting his hands roam up and down my body as I keep mine firmly in the warm dishwater. "She wants the recipe for the beef Wellington. I told her I'd get it to her."

My voice is light, but he knows exactly what I'm trying to do.

"You can give me the recipe, and I'll make a copy of it and give it to Eric. Or I can just give her that copy of it. You don't need to use it again, right? You made the recipe enough times you really should know the recipe by heart."

This is just him trying to get me all riled up. There are two things he wants right now. One, to keep me from being able to make contact with Carla to give her the recipe. Two, he wants me to flounder, to argue with him. He wants to hear me beg him to let me keep the recipe because we both know there's no way I could replicate dinner tonight without it. But I won't.

"I spilled some butter on it, I think. There's no reason to give her a recipe that's messy."

His hands tighten into fists, closing around the dress I have on. This simple action pulls the rest of the fabric tight around my body, and I suck in little sips of air. It's best not to let him know when I'm uncomfortable.

"Fine. You can type it up on the typewriter. Don't make mistakes."

"It would be so much easier to use the computer," I venture. He's in a good mood. We impressed his friends, and now they're going to tell everyone what a wonderful meal the four of us shared. It's what Zachary wants, for everyone to think he's perfect, and I pulled it off.

Maybe this time he'll let me use the computer.

"Lizzy, you know —"

It's dangerous to cut him off, but I do it anyway. "What if you disconnected it from the internet? Then I wouldn't have any chance to get online. You could disconnect it and let me type it on there, and then if I made a mistake, I could easily fix it."

"Yes, but if you made a mistake, then you wouldn't learn how important it is to be perfect, would you? Remember, if it's worth doing, it's worth doing right. How else are you going to learn that? Letting you rely on the computer like a crutch certainly isn't going to help you any." He releases the fabric of my dress but then grabs me by the hips, turning me so I'm facing him.

My hands drip water on the floor, and I hold them out from my body to keep from accidentally getting water on his suit. "I just thought it would be nice. It was such a lovely evening. And don't you think Carla will find it odd I was typing on a typewriter instead of a computer?"

"I think she'll find it quaint, like you have a little quirk she might not understand, but can think is cute. Like when people want to take up knitting. Or when they only drink from a special cup in the morning because they think it'll ensure they have a good day."

I'm not going to win this one. "Okay, you're right. I'll type it on the typewriter tomorrow."

"Tonight. I want to be able to take it to Eric tomorrow."

I don't have to look around to know how many dirty dishes there are piled up around the kitchen. And, as much as I'd like to pretend that I've gotten a lot faster at the typewriter since marrying Zachary, I always make at least a dozen mistakes before I get a perfect draft of whatever it is I'm typing up.

And I'm just so damn tired.

"It'll be ready for you when you come downstairs in the morning," I tell him.

"That's my good girl. Remember, wives are supposed to obey their husbands, right?"

I hate myself, but I nod. It's the best way to get through this. His little reminder of what a wife is supposed to be like and how she's supposed to defer to her husband is nightly. At first, I fought it, but what choice do I have?

He's taken my car keys. The Lexus I thought was a gift for me to drive whenever I wanted to was just for show. I can't go anywhere without him knowing about it, and not just because I don't have transportation. I'm not on the bank accounts, don't have access to my own money, and don't have a cell phone.

When I need to make calls, he's right there with me, the phone on speaker, his finger hovering over the red button that will end the call and cut me off from whomever I'm talking to. Zachary knows as well as I do that I don't have much of a choice in the matter of obeying him. He's made sure of that.

"Good girl. Clean this up; it's a mess. I want to hear you

working on the typewriter before I go to bed. I'm going to shower." Before leaving the kitchen, he wanders over to where he keeps some whiskey and pours himself a nightcap. The bottle he leaves on the counter with the cap to the side.

The message is clear. *Clean this up for me.*

And I'll do it.

As soon as he's out of the kitchen, I start cleaning faster, washing the dishes as quickly as I possibly can without breaking them. I've learned my lesson on cleaning up, and the pan I used to roast the carrots is lined with foil, making it easy for me to rip the foil off and throw it in the trash. I finish cleaning in record time, adrenaline helping me with my task; then I slip into the little office he made for me.

It's archaic. The centerpiece of my desk is an old typewriter he told me once belonged to his grandfather. A little cleaning and care and it would probably be in great condition, but some of the keys stick. Next to the typewriter is a stack of paper for me to use, and there's a wastebasket on the floor.

Three pictures hang on the wall in front of my desk. There's one of our wedding with him looking incredible, happy, handsome. I look tired, pale and thin, and the photographer had to do some sort of wizardry to add color back into my cheeks. Another photo is of him in his white coat. The last one is of me standing by the front gate of the house.

In this one, the smile on my face is real. I was stupid enough to think I was actually going to enjoy living here. I thought this place was going to be my castle, not my dungeon. It's gorgeous, sure, but I'm stuck here and can't get out. The last time I was in a car alone was ... well, when Margie broke down and he picked me up on the side of the road.

Giving my head a little shake, I put a piece of paper in the typewriter and spread the recipe out on the desk so I can copy it word for word. Normally I do my best to avoid the *F* key because it tends to leave a blob of ink on the page from time to time, but Zachary will check my work in the morning and make sure I didn't change a word from the recipe. At least there aren't that many instances of the *F* on the page I need to copy.

I start typing. At first, I loved the sound of the keys. They're so mechanical and sharp, the bright noise cutting through the silence as I type, but now I hate them. What I wouldn't give for access to a computer. It doesn't even have to be a nice one, just an old one I can use to type without second-guessing myself for a moment every time I'm about to press a key.

Half an hour later I've gone through four sheets of paper. I seem to make more mistakes when I'm tired, and right now I'm so exhausted I can feel my eyes closing of their own accord. But this time I think I have it right. I'm almost to the end, just to the part where you're supposed to rest the Wellingtons after baking so the meat doesn't lose too much of its juice when you cut them.

That's the mistake I made. I didn't have enough time to rest them, so some of the juice ran out of the filets when we all cut into them. I'm confident that's going to be one of the issues Zachary points out to me.

So close. Just a few more lines and I'll be finished. It will be perfect. I'll still get to bed at a halfway decent hour. Inching forward on my chair, I hunch over the typewriter. The muscles in my shoulders bunch. If I make a mistake now, then I'm going to beat myself up for twenty minutes about how close I was before I can start again.

"Are you finished yet?" Zachary's voice interrupts my thought process, and I pause, my finger over a key, unwilling to press it. "I must say, you've gotten better at using the type-writer, Lizzy, but you still make mistakes."

He leans over my shoulder. I'm still frozen, wanting to make sure I'm not going to make a huge mistake. I'm so close. So. Close.

"You're almost done, aren't you?" I smell the whiskey on his breath. "Well done, wife. You're becoming more perfect every moment you're married to me."

I'll kill you, you son of a bitch, just walk away and let me finish this.

Then I see his hand next to mine, his skilled fingers that save lives and make all of his patients love him. His fingers are *right there,* right next to mine, and then they're pressing down, his fingers jamming hard into three keys at once, slamming the letters up onto the page in a dark jumble that matches the hateful whirlwind tearing through my mind.

"Oh, God, look at that. And you were so close." He whistles through his teeth. "Looks like you need to start fresh, doesn't it?"

I don't answer.

I *can't* answer.

My chest feels tight. My heart races. It takes all of my self-control not to stab him with something, but what do I have in here? No scissors, no letter opener, no pen or pencil. Grabbing the edge of the desk, I take deep breaths, gulping down the air like a drowning man.

"You're getting closer to being perfect every single day, wife, but you're not there yet. Perfect is all that matters. Perfect wins. Remember that." He leaves the room, sucking all the air out with him.

I exhale hard and long, blowing all the air out of my lungs until they hurt.

Then I rip the paper out of the typewriter. Grab another sheet. Rest my fingers on the keys.

My hands can do this work while my mind works on the problem at hand.

I've killed before, and Zachary knows it. That's the secret he holds over me. That's the information he hopes will keep me compliant and willing to do whatever he asks of me.

Perfect is all that matters.

Yes, it does. He's right. My psycho husband who wants me to be nothing but perfect knows the secret that I already figured out.

Perfect wins.

He wants the perfect wife. The perfect marriage. The perfect life.

I want the perfect murder. Again.

10

BETH

I an walks the perimeter of the cabin, his footsteps loud on the wood floor. Mya, perched on the back of the sofa, is motionless as she watches him. Her unblinking gold eyes catch the light of the fire and reflect it. I have to tear my gaze away from her to watch my husband.

"It's got to be Ryan, I'm telling you, darling."

My husband, as confident as he sounds right now, has never once mentioned this man to me. I'd swear on it. Trying to look as casual and unconcerned as possible, I lean against the back of the sofa, my arms crossed for warm. "Who is Ryan?"

"The caretaker. He comes once a month for a weekend, moves in, and makes sure the place isn't falling apart."

"It's not the weekend." I'm being a bitch by pointing it out, but I can't help myself. I do manage to refrain from pointing out that Ian hasn't ever mentioned Ryan to me before. "If it is this guy, then why is he still here? Or maybe he forgot to lock the door, and someone else broke in."

He doesn't answer. Instead, he prowls, working his way around the rest of the cabin. Small as it is, he takes his time.

He's thorough. Safe. That's something I've always appreciated about him.

First the door, now the windows. He traces his fingers along them, jiggling locks, checking to see how secure they are. Now he pauses in the kitchen, his head on a swivel, taking in all the little details I failed to pay attention to earlier.

"Did you look in the refrigerator?"

I shake my head. It seems silly, like a joke, something he's asking to make me laugh, but his mouth is tight, lines appearing around his eyes. In one fluid motion he grabs the door and yanks it open, throwing it out to the side and stepping away like he fully expects something to burst out at him.

Nothing.

"What's in there?" Curiosity gets the better of me, and while I'd like to stay by the fire and try to shake off this chill that seems to have settled in my bones, I push away from the back of the sofa and walk into the kitchen.

"Nothing much. Some open jelly, ketchup. I doubt Ryan would have wanted to bring a lot out to the cabin and then carry it all back to the parking area when he came up." He frowns. "Beth, Ryan was here last weekend. He must have left in a hurry to leave his toothpaste and book here. If anything, he probably stayed a day or two later than normal. No big deal."

I hear it in his voice, the clear implication that he doesn't really think anyone is living in the cabin. It's in the way he said *no big deal,* like it left a bad taste in his mouth. He's trying to keep me from feeling like an idiot, but it's pretty clear to me that he thinks I'm overreacting.

But I'm not. How else would you explain all the little signs that point to someone making this place their home?

"And the cupboards?" I'm done waiting for him to poke around, and I turn, opening two at the same time.

Ian steps next to me, letting the refrigerator door shut with a soft thud.

"Pasta. Pasta sauce. Ramen. Canned beans, canned corn. Flour and sugar." I reach up, push a few cans out of the way. "Cat food." I frown, grateful my husband can't see my face. "Unless you left this all here the last time you were with your family, then I'd wager someone brought it with them. Someone who wanted to stay here for a while. And why is there a cat in here? Why did he leave her behind?"

He exhales. Standing as close to me as he is, I feel his breath on the back of my neck. He's still fully dressed for the storm outside, while I shed my coat when we came in. It's not that the small fire I built has warmed this place up enough for me to be hot, but I'm sweaty.

Anxiety, probably.

"Ryan must have moved all this stuff in. As for the cat, I don't know. Believe me, I wish I had an answer, but I just don't." He's not happy about admitting that to me, I can tell from his tone. "I'd call him if we had any cell reception, but there's no reception out here on a good day, much less during a snowstorm."

"And you really think he's gone?" I close the cupboards and turn to face him, crossing my arms before taking a deep breath. "Ian, I love you. Someone has been living here, and there's no way you can pretend that's not true. Ryan or not, someone moved in. If we can't be sure he's really gone —"

He frowns and takes a step back from me before running his hand down his face. "Someone was here, okay? Do I think it was Ryan? Yeah, probably, although he has a home. Not sure why he'd want to live here. But you're right, Beth, are you happy to hear me say it? There's no way they're going to try to come back now, not with us here." He shrugs like that settles it. "I own this place, and they'd be insane to try to get in now."

The newspaper. The date was from this morning. I open

my mouth to bring it up and see what kind of response Ian has about that, but the expression on his face makes me pause. He's tense, on edge. This isn't a side of him I usually see.

Yes, I know coming here to clean out the cabin has been stressing him out from the moment we talked about the trip a few months ago. That's why I promised him I'd come with him. Still, it's not fair for me to have to dance around what I really want to say to keep him from getting upset.

On the other hand, I don't want to get into it with him. Neither of us will come out a winner if we fight, so I drop it.

Instead I eyeball the window and don't answer. It's too dark outside to see anything, but I don't need to see how hard it's snowing to know it's freezing out there. Not a chance would I risk spending a night outside if I thought I could get someone to let me into their cabin for the night.

He gives his head a little shake, clearing it; then his gaze lands on Mya. "As for the cat —"

"The cat stays. Her name is Mya, and you're not kicking her out in this weather."

Ian has never had a soft spot for animals, which is something I've never understood. I love animals, grew up with dogs sleeping in my bed, and there's no way I'm letting him kick her out of the house and into that terrible storm. Mya might not be my cat, but I still owe it to her to protect her, and I'm going to do just that.

"Fine. The cat stays." He levels his gaze at me. "Did you have any problems getting the fire started?"

"The fire!" The words burst out of me — forget leaving things the way they were so I didn't stress him out. *I'm* stressed out, and that should count for something. While deciding what to tell him about the newspaper, I forgot to tell him the pièce de résistance, the final proof I have that Ryan, or whoever, didn't just *stay* here, they moved in here. "There were live coals. It didn't take much effort to get the fire going."

There. I want to hear how he's going to try to smooth this one over now. He might want to act like this is no big deal, but even if it's Ryan who was in the cabin, he wasn't supposed to be here.

"I already admitted that someone had been here, Beth." There's an edge to his voice that wasn't there before. "You have to trust me, okay? You're worried, but what do you expect me to do right now? Go looking for them in the storm? I need you to relax. Trust me."

I feel better, but only marginally. Is it common for people to squat in someone else's house or cabin when they're out of town? Maybe so. I never would have had the guts to do it, except when I was younger.

When you're desperate, you'll do just about anything to save yourself.

"Now, are you ready to eat? I'll make sure the door is locked." He must see the look on my face because he reaches out for me. Even though I don't really want him to hold me right now, I step forward, letting him wrap his arms around me.

Behind him on the counter is the slab of meat he carried into the house. I can see it over his shoulder, and I shrug out of his grasp. The meat needs spices, salt and pepper and garlic; then I can sear it and maybe finish it in the oven. I don't want to think about someone else in the cabin, and cooking is sure to distract me.

"You're right. I'll get started on dinner." On impulse I lean forward, give him a kiss, then step past him to start pulling open drawers until I find the spices I need. The drawer underneath it has an apron, and I pull it out but don't put it on.

"You going to wear that?" Ian turns to look at me from the

door. "You should, just to keep the grease from splattering on you."

"I don't know. Was it your mom's?" I don't know much about his parents since they both died before he moved to North Carolina and we met. I'm curious about the woman who raised him. She obviously wanted to make sure her son was smart and polite, thoughtful and resourceful. I finger the blue fabric, enjoying how smooth it is.

"Nope. Never seen it before. I'd wager Ryan brought it with him and moved it in for his weekends here." With that, Ian turns and leaves the room.

I shove the apron back into the drawer and slam it shut with my hip. It's one thing to wear his dead mom's apron. It's another entirely to wear something someone I've never met left in the house. Just the thought of it makes my skin crawl.

I'm in the middle of seasoning the meat when I hear a thud on the roof. Stopping, I look up, my hands chilled from handling the venison. "Ian?"

He doesn't respond.

The lights cut out.

11

LIZZY

I t's two months after we have the Havershams over for dinner that a letter arrives for me in the mail. It's not a joint letter, not one of those scams doctors and their spouses get targeted with when companies realize how much money is sitting in the bank account. It's a real letter, the paper creamy to the touch, my name written across the front in a gorgeous script. I know I should open it now, before Zachary gets home, but I sit on the floor by the front door and hold it in my hands, just smoothing it out over my knee again and again.

Normally we don't get mail dropped through the slot in the front door like this. It all comes to our mailbox, which is so far down the long driveway I can't even see when Zachary has raised the flag to let the mailman know they need to come by, but last week some drunk teenager took care of the problem for us. We'd been in bed, both of us on our own side of the king-size mattress, when the sound of squealing tires and a loud thud roused us from sleep.

Some sixteen-year-old with a new license had dipped into

his dad's stash of vodka, then gone for a joyride. He broke his arm — but what a lucky boy! — he was at the home of the venerable Dr. Pierce, who was able to check him out and make sure nothing else was wrong with him before calling 911 from the side of the road.

Of course, I watched this all from the bedroom window. Even though I couldn't see exactly what was happening, I could see the lights from the emergency vehicles, and then Zachary told me over and over how amazing it had been that he was able to help this poor, stupid boy.

As of right now, we don't have a mailbox. It's supposed to be installed this week, but the weather has been terrible, the ground too wet, and it feels like the universe is conspiring in my favor for once.

I flip over the envelope, well aware that I need to hurry up. Zachary will be home soon and will want to know exactly what came in the mail.

The flap pops up, and I pull out an invitation. It's to me, not to Zachary and me, and the thought of going anywhere without my husband thrills me. Of course, it will never happen. He'd never let me out of his sight long enough to go to a women's luncheon, which is what this invite promises. Drinks, lunch, and live music on the back deck. It's from Carla, the only woman I've spoken to in months, and that was just at our dinner here.

But she apparently likes me enough to want to include me in her luncheon. There's a number at the bottom, *her number*, giving me a way I can call her and let her know if I'm coming. The luncheon is next weekend, so I need to RSVP soon. I trace her number, rubbing my finger over every digit like I'm soaking it up. I commit it to memory.

When will I have unchaperoned access to a phone? I don't know that I will, but her number is mine now, and Zachary can't take it from me.

Zachary.

The thought of my husband coming home right now and stumbling upon me on the floor, crouched over this letter like Gollum, spurs me to my feet. I never should have opened it. I shouldn't have sat right here and read it on the floor. If anything, I should have left it for him to find. Eventually I'd have found out what was in it because he would have wanted to tell me just to torture me over the fact I'm not going to be allowed to go.

But now there isn't any way to hide the fact that I opened the letter. Even though I know it's useless, that the front door will be locked tight, I try the handle. A soft moan escapes my lips when it doesn't move. My mind flashes to the windows, to the glass, but I tried that once.

Keyword: once.

It's not regular glass, not like normal people would have in their windows. This glass is thicker, bulletproof, he claimed. It wouldn't matter how much I banged on the glass or how hard I tried to escape, there's no getting out of the house.

One thing I can say about my husband — he's very thorough. He thought it all out before bringing me into his home and made sure there wasn't going to be any way I could escape.

I lift the little letterbox door. On my knees, I crane my neck so I can look outside. The driveway is so long I can't see the road from here. From time to time, when I'm really quiet, I hear cars down there, but nobody ever makes the trip up to the house unless they have a good reason.

I could push the letter back through the slot. If I do it hard enough, then it's entirely possible it will end up far enough away from the door that Zachary might believe the mailman dropped it on the porch. He might think I didn't open it.

There's perspiration on my upper lip, and I wipe it away, letting the letterbox slot close. Or, with my luck, it would fall right outside the door, and Zachary would easily be able to figure out that I'd opened the letter.

Shit.

I glance down at my watch, a gorgeous Rolex Zachary bought me as a wedding present. It's huge, loaded with diamonds, and not my style, but he told me I had to wear it, so I do, even though I don't leave the house most days. I'm half-hoping I have more time before he'll be home, but according to my watch, I have less than five minutes.

That's another thing about Zachary. He's always punctual. It sounds crazy, but at least I know when he's going to be around, when he'll be showing up, when I need to make sure I look my best. He told me after we got engaged that he was going to have cameras installed. Of course, I didn't want it to be true, but he did it. Ugly black things, staring at me with blank eyes. Always on. Always watching.

I don't have time to change into something more comfortable, and while I'd love to strip out of the cashmere sweater and slacks I have on, it's not like I have any of my old, comfortable clothes to put on.

So I can't really break the rules when he's not here, but at least I know when to prepare myself for his arrival.

Before I can think things through, I'm up, running to the bathroom. The pile of mail is right where it fell through the letterbox slat, the invitation the only thing I took with me. I turn the corner into the guest bathroom and close the door behind me. The smell of rose soap is strong, and I gag, turning on the overhead blower, then kneel in front of the toilet.

I feel like I could throw up, but that's not why I'm here. My hands tremble as I rip the letter in half, then in half again. I turn it into confetti, making sure the pieces fall into the bowl and not on the floor. Even if months were to pass, if Zachary were to find a single piece of the invitation or envelope, he'd know what I'd done.

He'd figure it out.

I have to stay one step ahead of him if I can.

The surface of the water is littered with tiny pieces of paper, but I still have half of it to shred. My hand trembles as I reach for the handle.

"Please, dear God, go down."

The water swirls, a riot of pink, then drains, the toilet making a strange glugging sound. I know I should be worried about that, should reconsider what I'm doing, but I'm already tearing the rest of the paper into little pieces. They fall into the water, and I press the handle again.

It goes halfway down, pauses, bubbles back up.

"No, no, no. Shit!" Slamming my hand on the tank, I lift the lid to look at the water level. It's slowly filling back up, the level rising incrementally. I need it to fill completely before I can flush again.

It's close enough.

Another flush.

The sound of the alarm system going off. Zachary is home.

"Lizzy! Where are you?"

The water drains, the toilet gurgling unhappily. I'd love to plunge it, try to break up the mass of paper I'm sure is now lodged firmly in the pipes, but there isn't time.

"Just using the bathroom!" Spinning to the sink, I run the water and get my hands wet, then pat them dry on the towel. When I look up at myself in the mirror, I'm shocked at what I see.

I look exhausted. Dark circles have formed under my eyes. Sweat along my hairline makes me look like I ran a 5K.

"Come on out." It's not a request.

"Coming!" I turn off the water, look again at the toilet. It looks fine, and I don't think he'll be able to tell anything happened in here. Just as I'm reaching for the door, I see a bit of pink on the floor.

One tiny piece of ripped paper, about the size of a dime. Zachary's outside the door. I hear his footsteps stop there. Just that wood separates us.

I don't let myself think about what I'm doing. I bend, pick up the paper. Pop it in my mouth.

Make myself swallow.

"You know I don't like you locking doors. Don't make me take them off their hinges." The sound of a key in the lock, then the bathroom door swings open at me. I have to step back to avoid him hitting me in the face with it. He stares at me. "What were you doing in here?"

"I had to pee."

"You don't need to lock the door to pee. Is it that time of the month?" He's asking me questions but looking past me like he doesn't believe me. I'm half-afraid I might have left another piece of paper on the floor. I was careful. Right?

I can't turn around and look, though. He'd be onto me if I were to glance down at the floor by the toilet. I have to hope I got them all.

"I just had to pee," I repeat, sticking to my lie. The more I change it, the harder it will be to remember. My best option right now is to keep the same lie going for as long as possible.

"Fine. Well, I'm home now. Get me a drink. And dinner." He turns and stalks down the hall to the stairs, presumably to change from his work clothes.

I need to get a move on and do what he asked, but first I take a deep breath.

Hold it. Let it out.

I can't continue to live like this. Only one of us is going to make it out of this marriage alive. It was a dream before, but I have to make it a reality.

I have to kill my husband.

12

BETH

Once again I'm shining a light around the cabin, hoping that its thin beam will be enough to keep any demons that may be in this house at bay. I don't believe in monsters, not the type you can't see, anyway. This time I'm holding a flashlight, one of the superstrong ones designed for survivalists who need to be able to simultaneously light up half the woods and blind whoever might be coming for them.

I'll shine it right in someone's eyes if they come for me. That'll stop them in their tracks, give me time to think about what to do next.

People can be monsters, but I know how to deal with those and come out on the other side. Shortly after the lights went out, the fire did, too. It burned out faster than I would have thought possible, which tells me I didn't put enough wood on it. We need more, need it to be dry, need it to stay safe. Gone were the dancing flames that made me feel warm and safe and lit up part of the living room.

Now the entire cabin is dark.

Ian hovers at the door as he zips his coat all the way up. His fingers tremble a little as he pulls on his gloves.

Is my husband scared?

"I can go with you," I offer, but he laughs and shakes his head.

"My dear, the last thing I want is to put you in a dangerous position. You're much too precious to me." He pauses and yanks his glove the rest of the way on. "You stay in here and lock the door, okay? I don't want you getting hurt. Besides, it was probably just the wind knocking out the power. These things happen. I might not even be able to fix it right now, but I can at least go see what's happening out there."

I nod. What else is there to do? Ian believes I'm gentle, believes I'm incapable of taking care of myself, and telling him the truth in the middle of a blizzard isn't really how I thought the conversation would ever go. Sometimes we need to know the truth about our spouses. Sometimes it's better if we don't.

Besides, all he had to do was look into my past. He didn't.

That's his oversight, not mine.

"I'll lock the door," I tell him. "And I have my knife." It's in my pocket, and I pull it out to show him before I shove it back where it belongs, feeling like a little kid at show-and-tell in kindergarten. When he gets back in the cabin, I'll put it in my backpack so I don't lose it. "You be careful out there, okay? Come back to me in one piece."

"I'm not going on the roof to check the wires," he tells me, putting some of my fears to bed. "Right now I just want to see about hooking up the gas generator. Our power is gone, and there's no way to get it back in the middle of this storm, especially not when it's so dark out there."

"Okay." We're stuck here, on our own, and that means one of us has to go out into the dark to try to get the power back.

It's not that I'm unhappy about staying in the house, where there's at least a little residual warmth, but I'd be just fine outside. Still, this is what I wanted when I married Ian, isn't it? I wanted someone to take care of me, someone who was willing to put me first while they put themselves second.

It was hard for me to accept at first, that much is true. After spending my entire life being the only person I could rely on, it was a struggle to let him take care of me. Now, though, I like it. I love knowing that he's willing to do anything to help me out.

I love him more than I ever thought would be possible. If someone had asked me when I was a little girl if I would ever be married and be happy, I would have said that I hoped I would. Honestly, though, none of my dreams ever have come close to my real life now that I have Ian.

Ian disappears, and I close the door behind him, throwing the bolt to lock it. Unbidden, the thought that whoever has been living here probably has the key and could easily open the door enters my mind, but I shove that thought away.

Not helpful. Not now. Later tonight, when we have power back and are both in bed, then I can allow my imagination to run wild. Until then, I need to stay focused. I need to make sure I'm here to help Ian if he needs me.

Knowing how cold he'll be when he gets back in the cabin, I head to the fireplace to see if I can get the fire going again. It had been easy to stoke, but it had torn through the wood I put on it. We need more, or we're not going to be able to keep the fire going all night long.

There's got to be more wood out under the shelter, but until Ian is back, I'm not leaving the cabin. Right now I'll just have to make do with the wood stored in the house, and I add some to the fire, nestling it among the embers and blowing gently on the bright orange sparks.

The wood flares back up. "Thank you," I mutter, grabbing some more dry pieces and carefully setting them where they'll burn without blocking all the oxygen from the pile. "If I'm going to spend the night in this place, then we have to have some warmth, at least."

The fire roars back to life. I hope Ian will figure out how to get the generator working, but even if we can't take care of it until the morning, at least we'll have heat and light from the fire.

There's part of me that wants to stay here by the flames, crouched here in their dancing light like a goblin, to make sure the fire doesn't go back out. Instead, though, I feel called to make sure Ian is okay. He's doing a great job playing off that he's not concerned about whoever was in the cabin, but I'm worried.

I want to check on him.

Walking to the front door, I yank on my boots. Ian's out there in the dark and cold, and I love the man, but at this point in his life, he's much more suited to the classroom. He doesn't know how to handle someone who might be messing with us.

If it's Ryan, then I really want to know why he thinks this is funny. I don't understand, if he and Ian get along so well, why he would want to play with us like this.

Because that's what it feels like — like we're mice and he's the cat and he's batting us around until he gets bored of us. My main concern is what will occur when that happens.

As soon as I step out onto the porch, I know I've made a mistake. Earlier when I was worried about Ian, I considered coming out here before I realized I'd get lost. At that time there had been some residual light from the sky reflecting off the snow, but now everything is dark. Only the windows of the cabin show any light.

Taking my time, I pick my way down the stairs. The snow

on them is thick, with a layer of ice forming underneath from where we've compacted the snow. It's going to be rough going in the morning, but right now I'm just focused on getting to Ian.

"Ian!" Cupping my hands around my mouth, I call his name. "Ian, come back! We'll be fine without it!"

Nothing. The snow has slowed, although it's still coming down. Now, though, it's more like small icy pellets than the large fluffy flakes we were faced with earlier. They hit my face, each one burning with cold.

I have two choices. The smart one would be to go back inside the cabin and lock the door behind me. That's the one most people would choose.

But I want to make sure Ian is safe.

Even though I can't shake the feeling someone is watching me.

It's scary letting go of the stair railing, but I do it anyway and step out into the snow. Immediately, I sink up to my knees. It wasn't nearly this deep when we first got here, and I wince as the snow starts to melt through my jeans.

I can do this. I can do anything I need to.

"Ian!" Turning to the right, I start walking. The cabin is to my side, and I keep my eyes on the window, looking for the flashes of light from the fireplace. When I reach the edge of the cabin, however, I pause.

I can turn around the side of it and keep looking for him. Maybe I'll be able to help him. Slowly, I shine my flashlight in an arc along the side of the cabin.

No Ian.

But if I leave the front of the cabin, then there's a very good chance the squatter might come back. It suddenly hits me how stupid I'm being standing out here in the snow. Even if it is this guy, Ryan. Ian trusts him, that much is obvious, but what do we really know about him? I've never met the man, and I have no idea what my husband really knows about him.

I hate to admit it, but Ian is too trusting.

Ryan could make a run for the door and get in before I could even get turned back around. My feet feel like ice cubes. As much as I want to continue around the side of the cabin to see if I can help my husband, I turn back.

I keep telling myself I can take care of myself, and I have before.

But this feels different.

13

LIZZY

We're eating dinner when it finally happens. I could easily become a vegetarian, would love to eschew meat and all of the environmental problems I believe are tied to its production and consumption, but the one time I brought it up with Zachary, he'd laughed at me and told me to make three types of meat for dinner and to prepare myself to eat it all.

Wasteful. All of it. I thought he'd been joking that I was going to eat it all on my own over the course of a week, but he was serious. Now I poke at my filet, well aware that people all around the world would kill to be in my position and get to eat my dinner. Just the thought of dragging a bite of it through the homemade béarnaise sauce and then eating it is enough to make me feel like I'm going to be sick.

Instead, I poke at my sweet potatoes and take small sips of ice water, hoping he's not going to notice that I don't have much of an appetite. The pantry and the refrigerator have locks on them, so I'm not allowed to eat outside of specified times with him. From time to time, he's threatened locking me in the basement, where I won't have free range of the house during the day, but I always manage to placate him. Usually it's with tears.

He loves it when I cry.

Tonight it was with a delicious meal, one I knew would make him really happy. When I look up, I realize he's staring at me, a strange expression on his face, and I take a bite of meat. It's just a sliver. Hopefully it's enough.

"Did you have a good day at work?" Forcing a smile to my face, I try to pretend like we're a normal couple. That's what a loving wife would ask. Reaching up, I adjust my pearls, making sure they're lying just right across my collarbone. I look like the perfect wife. And as long as he thinks I am, he won't tell anyone my secret.

"It was a long day. Lost a patient on the operating table, but that's how it goes sometimes."

My stomach turns. I wish I hadn't asked.

He can see I don't want to know more, and a grin spreads across his face. Carefully, like we're in a fine restaurant, he puts his knife and fork down on his plate. Pushes it away. Stares at me. "Do you want to hear the details?"

"No." I shake my head, not daring to look him in the eyes. He loves finding any weak spot he can exploit, any way he can make me upset. "I'm sorry that happened, though."

"I'm not. He was a drunk. He didn't take care of himself, didn't contribute to society. He was on the table, things were going well, and then they weren't."

A chill races along my arms, leaving goosebumps in its wake. "What was the surgery for?" I don't want to ask, but there's a strange expression on his face. Something is brewing there, something he wants to tell me, but he wants to make me work for it.

"Just an inguinal hernia." A shrug. Casual. Uncaring. "But when we opened him up, he was just riddled with cancer. A less experienced doctor wouldn't have been able to see it, to tell what it was so quickly."

"Thank goodness you were the one operating." I doubt there was any cancer. I can see my husband, scrubbed and prepped, peering into this man's abdomen, pointing out invisible flaws others can't see. "It doesn't sound like he had much of a chance at all."

"He didn't." Zachary's leaning across the table now. Even though I know he can't get me, not without lunging across the plates and our glasses and grasping for me, I still lean back into my chair. I want to put as much space as possible between the two of us.

"Then I hope it was fast. Did he have a heart attack on the table?"

"He bled out." A pause. He runs his tongue along his lower lip, watching me. Measuring me. *Judging me.* "You know, it's pretty incredible how quickly your blade can slip when nobody else is paying attention to what you're doing. You're just moving along, making perfect cuts, fixing the problem and then whoops. There it goes."

I can't drag my eyes away from him. I don't want to look at this man ever again. I hate the way he's staring at me like he's excited to see how I'm going to respond. If I had any way to run, I'd get up. I'd leave. Flee the room, the house, the state.

I know how to run.

"That sounds terrible." He was waiting for me to say something. I take a sip of water, put the glass back down. Look at the spot between his eyebrows. I don't want to look into his eyes and know the truth.

My husband murdered that man.

"Like I said, he was a drunk. He got what he deserved."

The silence grows between us. I know speaking again is stupid, but there's a question on my lips I'm not sure I'm going to be able to avoid asking. Before I can wise up and stop myself, it's in the air between us.

"What did he do to you?"

Zachary laughs, a deep belly laugh. I haven't heard him sound that amused in months. "He lied to me. He kept the truth from me. So I killed him, Lizzy. How does that make you feel?"

I shake my head.

"You haven't been keeping the truth from me about anything?"

The invitation. I shake my head again. There's no way he can possibly know about it. Even if Carla reached out to him, telling him she invited me, he'll just think the invite got lost in the mail. I can't imagine he'll put two and two together, but ...

But looking at his face right now, I think maybe he already has.

"Last chance, Lizzy. Have you lied to me about anything recently?"

Oh, God. I want to tell him the truth on the off chance that he'll be merciful, that he won't hurt me. Still, he's tense, his muscles tight. He looks like a predator about to spring for its prey. Nothing in his body language tells me he'd be gentle or forgiving. Telling him the truth right now is quite possibly the stupidest thing I could do.

Except for maybe lying.

I'm still torn on what to do when he slams his hand down on the table. Our glasses shake, ice tinkling as the water sloshes.

"What the hell is this?" He's not yelling, *not quite*, but I wince anyway, fully expecting there to be a backhand attached to the way his voice rises with every word. "Tell me what this is!"

He lifts his hand, leaving behind a tiny piece of paper, a

little bit of pink confetti, one a bit larger than some of the others, this one the size of a nickel.

"Oh God." My voice is strangled, and I stand, pushing the chair back from the table. It tips over. Clatters to the floor. I don't turn around to pick it up because that would mean looking away from Zachary, and that would be suicide.

"I found this last week in the bathroom. The toilet has been acting up, but you probably knew that, didn't you?"

I don't answer.

He continues, his face turning purple. "And then Eric asks me at work if you received the invite from Carla, if you were going to go to her little party. How did you get the invite, I wondered. There's no way you can leave the house during the day. I made sure of it."

He's standing now, pressing down hard on his side of the table like he has to hold it to the ground. I just stare, frozen to my seat. Never in my life have I understood animals who stand in the middle of the road and willingly get run over when they see a car coming, but that's me right now.

I'm the deer. He's the Mack truck, the brakes cut, screaming around a corner. He's blinded me, the ground is rattling under his weight and fury, yet I can't seem to make my body move.

"Then I remembered the day I got home from work and the mail was already here, pushed through the slot on the door. Do you remember that, Lizzy?"

I don't respond, but he doesn't wait for me to, either. He just powers ahead, the Mack truck intent on smearing me across the pavement.

"So I thought, would my wonderful wife dare to hide something like that from me? I poked around after you'd gone to take a shower, and I found this. It was easy to call Carla, to tell her we'd received some mangled piece of mail, but it was impossible to tell what it was and ask her what color the stationery was.

Such a pretty pink, don't you think? All it took was me pulling up the footage from the cameras, and I was able to confirm what I thought. I don't know why I didn't check them that day. I guess I trusted you, wife. But I won't make that mistake again."

He's able to see me all the time. The knowledge makes me feel like I'm going to throw up.

With one finger he slides the confetti across the table towards me. It's a clear invitation to pick it up and pretend like I've never seen it before, but I don't move. There's no reason to try to continue this charade when we both know the truth.

"She sent you an invite. You got it, destroyed it, lied to me about it. What a shame, because I would have been more than happy to let you go if you'd just asked me like an adult and not acted like a petulant child."

"Really?" As soon as I utter the word, I know how terribly I've messed up.

His face, already dark, twists, and another laugh is ripped from his throat. He's up, coming around the table.

I scramble to my feet, knocking my water over in the process. It was still mostly full, and the water spreads, a flood across the white tablecloth. There's a small part of me wondering who will clean it up after all of this, but then his hand is on my arm, clamped around it like a vise.

"You lied to me!" He roars the words into my face. "I gave you this gorgeous house and everything you could possibly want, and you lie to me?" When he shakes me, my head snaps back before I can stiffen my body, try to protect myself. "I told Carla you're going to that party tomorrow, my dear. What do you think about that?"

I don't believe him, but hope rises in me. It's quickly extinguished.

"But it would be a shame if something were to happen to

you, something terrible that would prevent you from being able to see her and her friends, wouldn't it? Can you think of anything like that?"

I don't answer. He doesn't want me to.

"Oh, Lizzy, I have a surprise for you."

He's dragging me. Reaching out, I grab for the door frame, my fingers cramping as I hang onto it in a bid to keep him from taking me from this room. There's a certain knowledge rising in me that if I let him pull me from the dining room, I'm sincerely going to regret it.

"You think you're better than me!" He yanks, and my fingers slip. I cry out in pain, but he doesn't notice or doesn't care. His arms are around my waist as he hugs me to him, then walks me down the hall. "You think you're smarter and better, but you and I are the same. That man today, he deserved to die. I need you to understand that."

I whimper, trying once more as we reach the basement door to get away from him. He throws it open, holding me at the top of the stairs. One push and I'd tumble down them, definitely break a bone, maybe break my neck. He'd play the part of the perfect widow before finding some other pathetic girl to take advantage of.

"Just like your father deserved to die, am I right?" He must see the shock on my face. "Yeah, I figured that out after I met you. Did you think I wasn't going to look into who you were before I married you? That was a happy accident if I've ever had one. There you were, so pretty, in need of someone to swoop in and help you out. But for you to have a skeleton in your closet I could hold over you? I couldn't have planned it better. The police were too stupid to see that you killed your dad, but I have enough money to find out whatever I want." There's his face, ballooning in front of me, so close to me I can see the pores around his nose. "You and I are the same, Lizzy. But only in some ways. Don't forget how much better I am than you are."

He shoves, and I scream, pinwheeling my arms out in a desperate attempt to fly, to slow myself, to grab the handrail and hang on so this descent slows or ends, but there's nothing I can do to stop how I'm falling, and he knows it, just like he knows what I did to my father, just like he knows I'm so desperate to stay out of jail that I'd rather stay with him in this jail he's made for me.

There's a loud snap, and I feel like I'm looking down on my body for a moment, taking in the scene, trying to reconcile the sound I heard with the way I'm sprawled on the floor, then the pain hits me, and I'm back in my body, screaming.

14

BETH

The sound of an engine firing up startles me. My head jerks up, causing an immediate cramp in the side of my neck. Every part of my body aches, from my neck down to my feet, and I stretch out, trying to get feeling back into my fingers and my toes.

How long was I out?

The fire still dances merrily in the fireplace. Next to me, now staring at me like I ruined her life, is Mya. She yawns and stretches, then curls back up, sighing as she does. I couldn't have been asleep for long, not when I was so worried about Ian outside in the snow.

Then it hits me. I woke up, not because I rolled over or got enough sleep, but because I heard something. The light is on above my head, the glow of it so bright I blink to block it out.

"The generator," I mutter. My mouth feels gross, dry and sticky, and I rub my fists against my eyes as I stand. All I wanted was to sit for a moment to take a load off and try to relax while Ian was outside, but I must have been much more tired than I realized. I can only imagine how unhappy he'll be when he figures out I fell asleep instead of keeping an eye out for him.

Stumbling because my right foot is asleep, I hurry to the door. A moment later I hear stamping on the porch, a clear sign Ian is back. Without thinking, I reach for the door, ready to unlock it.

But then I stop.

"Hello?" My heart pounds in my chest as I lean my ear against the door. The wood is cool to the touch, and I want to pull back, but not until I know for sure it's my husband on the porch and not the squatter.

No response.

"Hello? Are you there?" I'm half afraid to say his name, like calling for him will accidentally summon someone else to be on the porch. It's stupid, just a superstition. I know you're not supposed to whistle in the dark, not supposed to write your name in red ink. I don't know a superstition about calling someone's name when you're not sure who's out there, but the silence from the porch makes me break out in a sweat.

"Beth, I'm freezing half to death out here! Let me in!" Ian's voice is muffled, but I still recognize it. Sighing with relief, I sag against the door for a moment, then fumble the locks, throwing it open. My husband practically falls through the door into the cabin. I step out of the way, closing the door behind him and locking it before I turn to look at him.

"You fixed it," I say, reaching for him and undoing his scarf. "We have light."

"Not for long, the gas is almost out." He shivers hard, his teeth clattering together. I thought that only happened in books and movies, but Ian's freezing and can't seem to control the movement. "I had to clean the snow off everything before I could even try to connect it. Someone has been messing with it."

"Go to the fireplace," I tell him, giving him a little shove in that direction. "Let me make you something warm to eat. How long do you think we have for the light?"

"Not very." He walks away from me, and I hurry to the kitchen. When he speaks again, his voice is raised so I'll be able to hear him. "There's not a lot of gas in there at all, so we don't want to run a lot of power. I don't know if it will make it to morning."

My stomach twists as I listen to him. On autopilot, I find the instant coffee in the cupboard and pour water in a pot to take to the fireplace. If he's serious about us running out of gas soon, then I don't want to use a lot of it to heat up this water. After he warms up, I'll see if I can heat up something for us to eat.

We're silent as the water heats. When steam rises from it, I pour it into a mug and stir in some coffee. The liquid instantly darkens, the scent rich. I hand it to him, and he takes a sip.

"Thanks."

We're silent for a bit longer. I'd love to know what he's thinking and if he has the same worry I do, but before I can gather up my courage to ask him if he's worried about the squatter, the light above us flickers and dies.

Instantly, the low rumble that had accompanied the light is gone as well. Silence descends on us, so fast and heavy that it feels like I've suddenly gone deaf.

"That much gas," he says, his voice low. "We had that much gas." He loudly slurps his coffee, then walks to the kitchen, putting the mug in the sink. He turns to me, and even though I can't see his face, I hear the exhaustion in his voice when he speaks. "I'm going to bed, Beth. You coming?"

I can't seem to answer him. Instead, I watch as Ian stands and stretches, the bottom of his shirt pulling up a bit and exposing a strip of skin. I could go to bed with him, and the two of us could stay warm. He'd curl around me like he does when he knows I've had a bad dream or am having trouble sleeping, and everything would be fine.

"I'm going to watch the fire." The words are out of my mouth before I even realize that's what I'm going to say.

Ian's facing me, the light from the flames reflected up on his face. He nods once, then turns for the bedroom, leaving the door open. It's a clear invitation for me to follow him.

Or he just wants to make sure he doesn't miss out on any of the heat from the fire.

The fact that he didn't try to keep me up talking and that he's so silent right now tells me just how upset he is. Ian doesn't usually hold back when he has something to say, which is one thing I appreciate about him.

I can only imagine how frustrated he is right now. He trusted Ryan to take care of the cabin, and now the man moved in, used the gas, and made himself at home. I wish there were a way to undo everything that's happened since we got here.

But all I can do is try to support Ian. It's not easy, not when he's so stressed out.

Standing, I walk to the front door, being careful where I place my feet so I make as little noise as possible. The silence is oppressive, the popping of the fire the only sound in the cabin, and I want to be able to hear if someone comes up to the house. After double-checking the locks, I return to the sofa, pulling a blanket up over me and curling into the corner of it.

There's a lumpy pillow, and I adjust it, staring into the flames before I close my eyes.

I'll just shut them for a few minutes. Just long enough to get rid of this pounding in my head. Then I'll put more wood on the fire and go join Ian in bed. That's what he wants, to have me here with him while we get this place ready to go on the market. I can do that for him.

I'm so tired that I can't help the way my eyes close. I can't help how my breathing deepens.

From somewhere outside the room, I hear a soft thunk.

Must be Ian, finally going to bed.

15

LIZZY

My neck aches. No, scratch that. There isn't a single part of my body that doesn't hurt, from my toes all the way up to the top of my head. I moan, and there's a hand on my cheek, caressing me. Without thinking, I turn into the touch.

"There's my girl."

Revulsion washes over me at the sound of my husband's voice. I try to pull away from him, but my head is supported by pillows. The best I can do is sink a little deeper into them, but his hand stays on mine, his skin so warm it should be comforting.

But it's not. He killed someone yesterday. Threw me down the stairs. *What kind of monster is he, really?*

"Why?" My voice croaks. My lips are dry. I lick them and try again. "Why did you do that?"

"Do what?" His hand pulls back from my cheek. When I force my eyes open, I'm not surprised to see him leaning over me, concern written all over his face. "Why did I take you to the hospital? You fell, darling. Right down the stairs."

I try to shake my head, but the pounding is too intense.

Closing my eyes, I focus instead on breathing. It's difficult for me to do much of anything but take in tiny wisps of air. Bracing myself, I try again. "You pushed me."

"No, you fell. You don't remember?" He brushes my hair back from my face. I cringe, but if he notices, he doesn't say anything. "You fell."

I don't respond.

"Say it."

"I could have died."

"You could have, and then I wouldn't have to deal with you ever again, would I?" His fingers press hard into my skin. I want to pull away from him, but there's no place to go, not in this little hospital bed. He has me pinned in, and he knows it. "Say it, Lizzy. Say that you fell."

My entire body hurts, but most of the pain is concentrated in my arm. While he waits for my response, I try moving my fingers, try to rotate my wrist. It's impossible, and I force my eyes open only to see a bright pink cast from my hand up to my elbow.

The bastard broke my arm.

"Say it now."

"I fell." My mouth is a traitor, but it seems to please him. Zachary sits back a bit from me. I didn't realize he's on the bed with me until I feel the mattress move with his shifting weight. He's so close, so loving. *The doting husband.*

"Atta girl. Thank goodness I was there to pick you up and make sure you got the treatment you need. I'll get you out of here soon enough and have you back home. Then I really can't wait to show you the surprise I have for you."

There's nothing for me to say. For a brief moment I consider crying out for help, but Zachary links his fingers through my good ones and squeezes them tight when the nurse comes in to check on me. I've been in a position like this before.

A powerful man.

Nobody to help you.

Only one way out.

The implication in his grip is clear. *Don't say a word; don't do anything to make the nurse think something is wrong.*

"Looks like you're good to go!" The nurse is happy, cheery. She's a ray of sunshine in this dark room, and I make myself smile at her. "You're so lucky to have such a great husband. Dr. Pierce will take care of you."

He'll take care of you.

Her words have an ominous tone, but I'm the only one who picks up on it.

Zachary shuttles me out of the hospital, to the car, into the house. He locks the door, tapping his cell phone to set the alarm.

I stand off to the side in the hallway, wary, my legs still feeling a bit like Jell-O.

Finally, he turns to me. Gone is the kind man who was perched on the edge of my bed. At least, he looked kind. I knew it was a mask as surely as I know now things are about to get very, very bad.

"You look terrible. Bruised from head to toe. I guess you can't go to Carla's party today, can you?"

The party. Of course, I knew he wasn't really going to let me go, but tears still spring, unbidden, to my eyes. "You pushed me so I couldn't go."

"What did you think was going to happen, huh? You think you'd be invited to this little party, you'd have a great time, maybe you'd let it slip that you married a monster? How many people in town do you think would believe you, Lizzy? I save lives. You were serving people overdone burgers and limp fries before I rescued you."

"Why are you doing this to me?" I hate crying in front of him. My arm throbs, the pain so intense that it makes me want to throw up. "Why were you so nice to me, and now you're so mean? What is wrong with you?"

"Wrong with me?" He's in front of me now.

I take a step back, feel the wall behind me.

"What's wrong with me? You killed your father and then ran away to Alabama, Lizzy. I think if anyone has explaining to do here, it's got to be you. Don't act like you're innocent in what's happening to you."

"He was abusive!" The words explode out of me. "That doesn't give you an excuse to hurt me."

"No, but it does give me a really good way to trust you'll never try to turn on me. What are you going to do, tell the police? I'm sure they'd love to lock you up for the rest of your life. Come on, you knew this was how it was going to play out. Now, darling, I want you to go into the basement. It's perfect for you down there."

"No." I won't. Keeping my injured arm as close to my body as possible, I try to scoot past Zachary, but he's faster than me. He pins me against the wall, his hands planted next to my head. His breath is in my face. He's been chewing gum, and it smells like peppermint. "No, Zachary. I won't."

"Come on, wife, I made it for you. I wanted to show you last night, but you were just so clumsy you didn't get to see it." He bends his knees. Wraps his arms around me. Scoops me up. I'm tight against his chest, unable to free myself.

Without thinking about what I'm doing, I bring my arm down on his shoulder. He hisses as the cast strikes him.

Bright light flashes in my eyes as pain explodes, shooting from my arm through my entire body. It feels like I'm on fire, like I'm going to break apart, lose my arm, pass out. I scream. My eyes are closed, my body limp.

Zachary doesn't stop moving. I'm vaguely aware that he's carrying me, hurrying to the basement door, but I can't move.

Each step he takes sends another throbbing pain through my arm.

"It's all perfect," he tells me. "Perfect, perfect. You're going to love it. It's just like what my father did for my mother. He loved her so much, just like I love you, and he wanted her to be perfect. He made her beautiful, you know. Just like I'm going to do for you. That's what we do for the people we love. We make them perfect."

He pauses, and I take a deep breath, ready to scream. But who would hear me? Nobody lives near us, and I can't hope for a moment that anyone would come running. Before I can decide what to do, he continues.

"Except for my brother. He doesn't like to make things perfect. He likes to destroy them. We seem to be opposites, Lizzy, but he and I are still a lot alike. You'd be surprised how similar we are. That's why I came to Alabama. I needed someplace small where I could find someone to fix. I found you."

I'm half-listening to him. There's part of my brain screaming at me that I need to escape, but how am I to do that when he's not letting me go? Even if he were to put me down, my legs would give way. The only thing I know right now is pain.

And fear.

And the sense of darkness pressing down on me.

"Here you go, Lizzy." Zachary's voice is almost kind, and I open my eyes, a stupid spring of hope rising in me that this was all a misunderstanding, that he made a wonderful room down here for me, that he doesn't want to hurt me.

But even without looking around me, I know I'm wrong.

"Oh, God." My good fingers curl into the blanket covering the mattress he put me on. I shy away from him, lifting my feet up from the floor and pulling my knees into my chest in a bid to make myself as small as humanly possible. "Oh, God, what are you going to do to me down here?"

"I'm going to make you perfect." Pleasure swells in his voice. It's been a long time since I've heard him sound this excited about anything, and even though a good wife, under normal circumstances, would be happy to hear her husband so pleased ...

It terrifies me.

"Zachary, please, no," I say, scooting farther away from him. I don't want to look around the basement and see what he has planned, but I can't help the fact that my eyes flick around the space while I wait for him to respond. I'm in a bed, twin size, with metal rails. It takes me a moment to place where I've seen one before, and then it hits me.

I'm in a hospital bed.

There's a small table next to me with a tray on top. Gleaming silver instruments are on the surface, each of them placed equidistant from the ones next to it. I recognize some from watching movies, but I can't name a single one. All I know is that I don't want any of them near me.

Just like I don't want my husband near me.

"You're a psycho!" I scream the words at him, holding my casted arm close to my chest. "What the hell is wrong with you?"

"Nothing." He holds his hands up like he's trying to show me he's not a threat. "Nothing. I just know you had a hard life. I picked you up off the side of the road, for God's sake. I thought you'd like to be perfect. My father did it for my mother. It was a gift, even though she didn't see it at the time. My brother and I didn't see it at the time. But she grew to appreciate it. And now I see what a gift it was. Why wouldn't you want to be perfect?"

It hits me. The control. The way he carefully monitors every interaction I have with other people. How hard he works to make sure I never make a mistake, especially when we're around other people. Which, to be fair, isn't very often. He's done a wonderful job controlling me and making sure I don't embarrass him.

This is just the next step for him.

"I just want to be normal," I say, reaching for him with my good hand. My wedding rings are gone, and I start, staring at the finger where they're supposed to be. He doesn't like it when I take them off. Did I do that and just forget? Am I going to have to deal with him about that now?

"I took them off at the hospital so you didn't lose them." Lifting a chain from around his neck, he shows me the two rings there. The diamond flashes in the light from the overhead bulbs. "The last thing I wanted was for you to lose them." He drops the chain, and the rings disappear from sight. "Now, do you want to make a big splash the next time people see you, or do something smaller? I have friends who will come help me. Doctors I can pay to fly here, to fix you."

"Something small." My voice shakes. If he notices, he doesn't remark on it. "Please, Zachary, please, if you're going to do this —"

"I am. We'll start with something small, wife, and you'll see that I'm just doing this because I want to help you. That's all there is to it. I want to help you, to make you perfect. We can do something small; you'll see I'm on your side. Then we can fix you."

He reaches out, strokes my cheek, then grabs my chin, turning my head so I'm looking to the side.

"Your nose. Your breasts. You've gotten thin, Lizzy, and they need to be perky. We can get you transplants, shave a bit off your nose. A face-lift. Any excess skin, gone. Anything you hate about your body, removed, repaired. Don't you see what a gift this is? Any woman in your position would be thrilled to be able to fix themselves. That's how much I love you."

I have no idea how I'm going to get out of this, but there's no way I'm going to rot down here in this basement and let him torment me. Swallowing hard, I look up into his eyes. "Can we do something really little first, but something that's been driving me nuts?"

"What is it?" There's so much compassion in his voice. It disgusts me.

"I hate my hair." It's a lie. I love my long blonde locks. "It's brassy. Can you fix that, just to let me see how easy this can be? How good it will feel?"

He pauses. For a moment I think he's going to agree, that he'll allow me to choose what hell he's going to put me through. It's a silly hope and one that's dashed with his next words.

"You don't really think I went through all this trouble just to change your hair, do you?"

16

BETH

The crick in my neck is back, this time with a vengeance. I open my eyes, slowly at first, blinking against the light as I struggle to remember exactly where I am and what happened last night. The small cabin is flooded with light, and I feel a surge of hope in me that Ian must have fixed the lights while I was asleep.

Turning slowly, my hand pressed against my neck, I look around the room, then up at the overhead light. It's still out. The light flooding the room streams in through the windows. It's still early, or feels like it is. I'm not surprised to see light reflecting off the snow when I make my way to the window to look out.

The glass frosts under my breath as I stand there, and I reach out, carefully wiping it away. I don't think I've ever seen snow like this.

North Carolina snow doesn't come on so heavy or fast. Sure, there was that one blizzard back in 1993 that all the locals love to reference like it was a big life-changing event, but I've never seen snow this deep. It's mounded, piled high, bending tree branches so low they seem like they're going to break.

Turning away from the window, I massage my neck, then put more wood on the fire. The bedroom door is still open, but I go to the bathroom first, desperate to relieve myself and to brush my teeth. Thank goodness there's running water — I'm sure the cabin is on a well, but I have no idea if the source will freeze up in this cold weather or not.

Digging through my backpack, I find some painkillers and pop them. I'm going to be pretty useless helping Ian clean up the cabin with my neck hurting like this. Although, to be fair, I don't think we have a lot of work to do.

Ryan has kept this place really nice.

It still bothers me how flippant Ian seems about the man he hired to take care of this place. It may be silly, but I'm determined to find out more about Ryan and what my husband knows about him. Maybe that will put my mind at ease about this entire thing.

Then Ryan will come get Mya. He'll leave, and Ian and I can do what we came to do. When the cabin is all cleaned up and ready to be put on the market, we'll leave, the place will sell, and I'll never have to think about this trip again.

Satisfied with my plan about how the day is going to go, I walk into the bedroom. Ian's stretched out in bed, his arm slung over the edge of the mattress, his mouth open as he softly snores. He's never been a super early riser, so I'm not surprised he's still asleep, although I do wish he'd get up so we can start the day.

I see his camera on the dresser. He'll want to get outside and take some shots of the cabin with this much snow around it, I'm sure of it.

Sitting on the edge of the bed, I reach out and lightly touch his shoulder. "Ian."

He stirs, and I call his name twice more before he finally rolls over, his eyes taking a moment to focus on me.

"Beth, I never felt you come to bed."

There's no way I'm admitting to him that I spent the night with Mya instead of with him. I smile, then brush some of his hair back from his face. It's starting to go a little gray around the temples, but nobody could ever look at my husband and not say he's attractive. There's something about the little gray combined with his sharp jaw that gives him a bit of a George Clooney look.

"Did you sleep good?" I ask, flipping back the covers so I can get in next to him. He's warm, and I scoot over to him, wrapping my body around his. "You were warm enough?"

"A little chilly," he admits. "But I think I can survive here a few more nights while we get everything taken care of."

My heart falls. *A few more nights?* I really thought he'd have the same thought I did this morning, which was that the cabin is obviously in pretty good condition and we can just leave. Sure, we'll have to make sure the roads were scraped last night before we can leave, but ...

He's staring at me, clearly expecting a response to some question I didn't hear.

"I'm sorry, Ian, what did you say?"

"I said that I want to get some shots of the snow around here and look for what problem we're having with the electricity. Barring being able to fix that, I need to walk to the car today and see if the roads have been touched. They usually treat them so the snow will melt off fairly quickly, or there might have been a plow through here already. If I can get out, it'll be easy to get enough gas to turn the generator back on. The fire is great, but there's no way we can rely on that for all our light and heat."

"You really think we need to stay?" My heart sinks. "This place looks great, Ian. Sure, it needs some touches, but we could easily hire a handyman to do that for us or sell it as is. What do you think we need to do around here? We can hire someone to fix whatever the electrical problem is, right? Or won't the company send someone to repair it?"

He shrugs, sitting up. I have to move away from him to give him space, and I have a feeling he wanted me to stop touching him. "I don't know, Beth. We both have the week off to be up here cleaning this place up, right? My school is closed for break, and it's not like a lot of people order flowers in the winter. So why not make the most of it? Just because we don't have a lot of work to do doesn't mean we can't stay and really enjoy ourselves. Think of it this way — we were going to work our butts off for a week. Now we just get to hang out, eat good food, enjoy the snow." He reaches out, lightly tracing down my arm before linking our fingers together. "We can enjoy each other."

I stiffen. Force myself to smile at him. "Ian, someone was living here." Why doesn't he seem to get this? "You don't think they'll come back in the next week? That snow out there is insane. They could be on the front porch, just waiting to be let in. I want to know about this Ryan guy you hired. What if it's him? What if he's trouble?"

Ian just shakes his head. I'm dismissed.

"No, whoever it was has to know they messed up being here. I appreciate them keeping this place picked up, but come on. They were in the wrong. Besides, Ryan is great, and I really think it was him. He's never been a problem the entire time he's been working for me, so why would he start now? Maybe he just needed a few nights away from home and then lost track of the days. I'm not going to get mad at him for that." He sounds so confident in himself, in the fact that nothing bad will happen here, that I want to laugh.

"So you know the guy?"

"Ryan?" He pauses and then tries to talk fast, like that will cover his momentary silence, but I know what I heard. "You don't need to worry about him."

"So you don't know him."

"I've never met him, no." I raise my eyebrows and pull away from him, making him speak faster. "But trust me, Beth, he's a good guy. I vetted him online, okay? What was I supposed to do, fly up here to meet him? He was thrilled with this job and obviously has kept the cabin in pretty good condition. We'll have someone come out and change the locks before we put it on the market, but honestly, I'd trust the guy to throw the key away if I asked him to."

"But Mya. Whoever was here is coming back. No matter if it's Ryan or someone else —"

"And I'll deal with that when the time comes." He pushes the covers off his body like he's ready to move, but I don't shift position. *We're having this conversation. Now.* He was too tired to have it out last night, and I wasn't going to push it, but now I want answers to my questions.

"Ian, seriously. Someone could get really mad. They could do something dangerous."

"What do you know about danger?" He laughs and pushes me out of the way so he can get out of bed before changing quickly. I know by the way his gaze lingers on me what he wants to do, but I'm not in the mood. Not when someone was messing with us last night. "Beth, take a deep breath. Someone was here. It had to be Ryan. I told you I'd call him, but —"

"Yeah, there's no service. I know."

"You're right, he'll probably come back for the cat, but then he'll leave again. I don't know where he was last night, but I'm not going to worry about that. I'm just going to put my head down and work through what we need to do to get this place looking great so we can put it on the market. Remember why we're here."

That was a low blow. It was his idea to sell the cabin to pay for IVF, his plan to come up here and fix it up so we can get the most money possible for the treatment. Ever since we got married, he's wanted kids, a houseful of them. The problem is me, not him, and I can't help the guilt I feel knowing I'm the reason he's not already a dad.

I came along on this trip because it was the right thing to do, but now I wish I'd stayed home. Everyone on social media told the two of us how lucky we were to take a trip together, calling it a *baby moon* like there's already a baby.

God, sometimes I really hate people.

Not that I want to bring my husband's social media habits into this. He's happy to share every detail of our lives online, while I'm much more private about things.

Right now, though, that's neither here nor there. I don't know how to make my husband take this more seriously, not when he seems so chipper about the entire thing. Sure, I understand he's got to be happy about not having to be at the high school teaching photography all week, but it makes me nervous to think about someone outside the house.

I just wish he would take it more seriously. Then again, Ian has never had anything bad happen to him in his life. He's one of the lucky ones.

"I'm going to start some coffee; then I'm heading to check the power line. If I can't fix it and have to get gas, I'm at least planning on getting some shots of this snow on the way to the Prius. Smile for me." He's gotten out of bed to grab the camera I saw earlier, one of his favorite old film ones. Then he snaps a picture of me before I have a chance to adjust my expression.

Yeah, I'm sure that one will be a keeper.

I'm still sitting on the edge of the bed, trying to wrap my mind around what he just said, when it hits me. "What did you say?" I rush out of the bedroom and come up behind him in the kitchen. "You're not really leaving here, are you?"

He doesn't answer until he fills a pot with water; then he turns, smiling at me like he doesn't see the problem. "Did you think I was joking? Beth, we need to fix the power lines. If I can't do that, then I need to get gas. There's an old sled in the shed where I skinned the deer. I'll load it up and walk back to the gas station to get what we need if the roads aren't clear enough to drive. This isn't optional."

"You'll be gone hours." I pluck at his sleeve as he walks to the fireplace. "You can't be serious. Why don't we both just leave, find a hotel with actual power, then get out of here?"

For a moment, he doesn't answer; then he shakes his head. "Beth, listen. I know you didn't really want to come —"

"I came because you wanted me to."

"Right. And I appreciate that. But I have the time off work. This is going to be my last time in this cabin before it becomes someone else's." His voice is tight, but I'm not going to let him prey on my emotions. Not now. "I want to enjoy my time here, not worry about Ryan showing up or huddle around the fireplace the entire time in a bid to stay warm. You understand that, don't you?"

I understand that he's being an idiot. "I'll come with you."

"Now, Beth, don't be silly." He settles the pot in the coals and blows on them before standing up and pulling me into a hug. Normally I'd melt right into his embrace, but right now I feel stiff, and I pull back as soon as he relaxes his grip on me. "You stay here where it's nice and warm. Lock the doors if that will make you feel better, but I won't be far. I know you're worried about someone coming to the cabin, but you need to relax. Besides, I'll just be around the house for a bit checking the electrical lines before I give up and go get gas, okay?"

He's a nice guy, he said about Ryan. But he doesn't even really know the guy.

Why doesn't he get it? Why doesn't he see that it's not just that I don't want to be here? I've never seen my husband this stubborn before. He just wants to do this, and he's not going to let anyone stop him.

"Fine," I say, because what other choice do I have? I could battle it out with Ian, but the man is used to getting his way, and I have a very strong feeling he's not going to back down now. "I'll be here when you get back from playing lineman. Don't get electrocuted."

"You're the best." He kisses me on the forehead and then checks the water. It's simmering already, the embers having sprung right back to life. "I'll pop this in a thermos and head out. Hey, if I do have to head out for gas, I'll have room on the sled so I can grab some gas station snacks and bring them back. It'll be a proper vacation. How would you like that?"

"Right. Sounds great." My voice is flat, but he doesn't notice as he prepares to leave. When it's obvious how serious he is, I put some cat food on a plate for Mya, then open the door for her to escape outside. She walks onto the porch, picking her paws up disdainfully once she sinks into the snow, then beelines back into the cabin. Her litter box is in the bathroom, and I'm not surprised to see her disappear through that door.

Just me and the cat, then. And a knife. It's in my backpack, but easily accessible.

Ian leaves, kissing me once more before reminding me to lock the door. He's in such a good mood to get out of the cabin and start trying to fix the electricity that he fails to notice the tracks outside the kitchen window.

But I don't.

17

LIZZY

My new nose snubs up at the end like a little ski lift. The tip used to be crooked, to have a bit of a tilt to it, like I'd gotten punched in the face when I was younger even though I don't remember anything like that happening. Now, though, it's perfect. I look like I walked out of a magazine.

Or my nose does, anyway.

"You know, Lizzy, you really should share the name of who did your nose for you." Carla tips her glass of wine in my direction. Instinctively I raise my own; then we both take a sip. "It's perfect. Don't you think, Eric?" She turns her head so her husband is looking at her profile. "What do you think, should I get mine shaved down a little bit?"

I know better than to answer her question about what doctor did my new nose.

As if on cue, Zachary clears his throat. "I had an old friend from medical school take care of Lizzy for me. He owed me a favor from back in the day, so it was really nice to be able to cash that in. She's been wanting her nose taken care of from the day we met, haven't you, darling?"

He puts his arm around me, resting his hand on my shoulder. From where Carla and Eric sit across from the two of us, they can't see the way his fingers dig into my skin.

Agree with me. Let them think you wanted this, and I gave you what you wanted. Tell them I'm the perfect husband.

"It was a lovely thing Zachary did, letting me get my nose done." I stare at Carla, trying to read the expression on her face. Are she and her husband really buying this? Do they honestly think I'd hate myself enough to willingly go under the knife?

She takes another sip of wine. Her eyes lock on mine; then she laughs, turning to Eric. "I know what I want for Christmas." She looks back at Zachary. "Do you think I could have his name? Your friend? It's so good. So smooth." She leans forward, getting a better look at my nose.

I want to stand and scream that they've got it wrong, but I just smile, my mouth tight.

Zachary's fingers are still on my shoulder, a constant reminder that I'd better not do anything to upset him. To embarrass him.

"I'll see about passing it on." Zachary's noncommittal. "Now, do either of you want something else to eat? Lizzy here has been saving the best for last. Haven't you?" He squeezes my shoulder one more time.

Don't mess this up.

"Of course." I stand, a little wobbly on my feet thanks to the wine we were sharing. I don't remember the last time I sat and drank more than half a glass of wine, but today I feel dangerous. I let Zachary do something terrible to me, and although I can't undo that, I can stop him from doing more in the future.

Right? He's the one who keeps throwing the fact that I killed my father back in my face. It's like he thinks I won't do it to him, too. Won't find him when he's weak, won't stop him from hurting me or anyone else ever again.

I'm in the kitchen, a large knife in my hand. I need to cut the cake I made, but all I can do is stare at the door that leads to the dining room. What would Carla and Eric do if I were to run in there, the knife over my head, and bring it down on Zachary? Would they try to stop me?

Or would Carla just scream and Eric stand there, useless, knowing full well that Zachary brought this on himself, that he's evil, that he deserves everything he's getting and more? I can't be the only person who doesn't fully understand what a terrible person he is. I can't be the only one in the world he has fooled.

"Lizzy, are you okay?" Carla peeks into the kitchen, her hand on the doorframe, a worried expression on her face.

I realize with a start I'm holding the knife like a murder weapon, and I laugh, adjusting my grip.

I turn to the cake. Away from her. I don't want her to see what was in my eyes. I don't want Zachary to be able to look back on footage from this later and know I was thinking about rushing through the house to kill him in front of our friends.

"I just got lost in thought, I guess." The tip of the knife sinks easily into the chocolate frosting. There are layers of thick chocolate frosting, ganache, and glacé cherries in between layers of Dutch chocolate cake. Chocolate curls decorate the top. Those bastards took me an hour to do this morning.

"You looked like something serious was on your mind."

I cut a slab of cake, put it on a plate. Wipe the blade so the second slice looks perfect. Cut another.

It's only now that I trust my voice enough to speak. "I'm fine. Just tired from being up all morning baking this cake."

She's next to me. So close I can almost feel the heat

coming off her body. I shift away, wanting to put space between the two of us. If Zachary were to look in here right now and see the two of us standing like this, he might think I was saying something to her.

"You sure put a lot of pressure on yourself to make everything perfect all the time. I don't know how you do it."

Another slab of cake. My hand shakes as I process what she just said to me. She thinks I'm the one demanding this perfection while she couldn't be more wrong.

"I just want it to all be perfect for Zachary." I speak louder than necessary. It's entirely possible he's come into the kitchen behind the two of us. He's quiet, I've learned that much. He knows how to move without being detected if he wants to watch me.

"Well, you're a better wife than I am. I would have just run down to the grocery store and picked something up. That's what I do all the time, actually. If you put it on a platter and kinda mess up the frosting a little bit, it looks completely homemade."

The grin she gives me is infectious, but I don't smile back. How am I supposed to pretend to be happy right now when the one person I prayed might be able to see the truth of what Zachary is doing to me clearly has no idea? He managed to hide how psycho he is from me because I was falling in love with him. This entire time I've been hoping she's not going to think he's as wonderful as I did.

My hope is for nothing.

"Well, Zachary's worth it." Loud again. So he can hear me.

Grabbing the serving tray with the four slices of cake, I turn around, only to almost run into Zachary. He's smiling, the small smile he gets when he's really pleased with what I've said or done.

"I'll take those, darling. I'd hate for you to trip and hurt yourself falling."

My smile slips.

"Oh, that's right, I forgot you'd broken your arm, Lizzy! What a nightmare to have that happen in your own house. You're so lucky Zachary was here to take you to the hospital right away. Can you imagine what would have happened if he hadn't been here? How does your arm feel? All healed up?"

"Oh, everything is perfect." I don't look back at her as I follow Zachary into the dining room. "Like you said, what would have happened if Zachary hadn't been here?"

I wouldn't have broken my arm, for one.

I wouldn't be walking on eggshells around someone.

How the hell he found out about what happened with my father is beyond me. He's smarter than I gave him credit for, that's for sure. More driven. More focused.

But my father thought he was smart, too.

And look where he ended up.

18

BETH

I an looked back over his shoulder once to wave at me before disappearing around the side of the house, a surprising pep in his step, his hands shoved into his pockets. He walked quickly, cutting through the drifts of snow that had slid from the roof and landed in soft piles. Even though I know I would have only slowed him down, and I don't know anything about electricity, I still wish I were out there with him.

At the same time, though, I'm warm. I have a cup of terrible instant coffee and a roaring fire. It's warm enough in the cabin that I've stripped out of my puffy coat and long sleeves and have on a tank top. From the window, I'm eyeballing the tracks I see disappearing into the woods.

He never saw them. I know he didn't. Ian isn't the type of man to avoid his problems, right?

And I'm not that type of woman.

"This is insane," I mutter, putting down my coffee and pulling my layers back on. I can stay in this nice warm cabin and pretend, like Ian, that everything is fine.

Or I can find out the truth.

It takes me a moment to pull on my boots; then I slip on my sunglasses to protect my eyes from the glare and stare out at the snow. The terrible wind from last night is gone, replaced by an eerie stillness that makes me nervous. It's one thing to experience a storm with all its power and rage.

It's another entirely to stand in its aftermath and feel the silence in your bones.

The air is cold when I push outside, the snow deep where it blew up onto the porch.

I no longer have the excuse of losing myself in the dark, so I leave the porch and walk straight over to the footprints. They're clean holes punched into the ground, the boots that made them larger than the ones I wear. I can clearly see the tread in the track, and that tells me whoever was here came after the snow stopped.

Not whoever. *Ryan.* Ian believes the person who left so many things in the cabin is Ryan.

But then why wouldn't he just come up to the house?

I wonder if he looked through the windows. Saw me sleeping on the sofa. The thought gives me chills.

Fully creeped out now, I hurry to the shed. The snow in here isn't nearly as deep, although a few inches managed to blow in. I can clearly see the tools hanging on the wall that, last night, were so difficult to make out.

But that's not all I see. To my right is a small table where Ian was gutting the deer. I remember helping him get the carcass on there, but there's no way I ever would have thought he'd have enough time to fully gut and trim the deer.

The head of it is pointed in my direction, the skeleton splayed out behind it. The meat has all been cut away, the hide removed and hauled off to God-knows-where. It's jarring, the red snow around the table, how drops of blood have flung out from the carcass in a dizzying circle, how the whole thing looks like some low-budget Pollock demented art project.

"Oh, my God," I say, taking a step back. I think back to how long Ian was out here last night, and try to make it all make sense.

I did fall asleep for a bit. Was it long enough for him to fully dress the deer? I have no idea how long that would take, but I can't imagine it's a quick process, especially not when it's so cold out and your fingers wouldn't want to work.

Forcing down my revulsion, I take a step closer to get a better look. The bare bones are so neat, without any knife nicks in them. It's hard for me to imagine my sweet husband, the man who works with angsty, artsy teenager photographers every single day, out here wielding a knife and carefully cutting meat from bone, sinew from muscle.

And for him to be able to do it so perfectly.

How well do I really know him?

Fear takes hold, and I stumble back from the deer. It can't hurt me — I know that. The man who dressed this deer is gone, back around the side of the house, trying to figure out what happened to our electricity last night.

Unless.

My mind doesn't want to go there, but I know I need to.

Unless the person who dressed this deer, who took his time with it, who made perfect little cuts and worked with the carcass in the middle of a storm ... unless it wasn't Ian.

Unless it was Ryan. The squatter. I have to believe they're one and the same. Otherwise I think I might lose my mind, might start conjuring up half a dozen people staying in the cabin, watching us.

But why would he have dressed this deer, so close to the cabin, without letting us know he was here? Why wouldn't he knock on the door, look for shelter, ask us to let him in? The storm was terrible. Nobody in their right mind would want to be out in it, but nobody came to the house last night and asked us to let them in.

I would have heard it. I'm sure of that.

So what does this all mean? I glance once more around the shed. Last night I missed all of the details in my hurry to get inside. I barely noticed the cords of dry wood, the old tools hanging on the walls. I hadn't really seen the pliers, the saws, the weed eater all stored until spring. Now I look at them, letting my mind wander as I try to make sense of what's going on.

It's almost impossible. It's one thing for me to try to wrap my mind around the thought that someone has been staying at the cabin even though they weren't supposed to. Ian obviously hired someone he trusted to take care of the place every once in a while, but it's strange to me that he's not really worried that the guy has clearly been sticking around longer than he was supposed to.

Then again ... I love my husband, but he's never dealt with anything difficult in his life. Never once has he had to handle someone who might want to hurt him, someone who doesn't like him. He's damn likable, which is why I fell in love with him in the first place.

It also means he's a bit more trusting than maybe he should be. I love that about him — or I did up until this very moment when I'm suddenly wondering what kind of person Ian hired to take care of the cabin in the first place — but that's not always a good quality to have.

He doesn't seem worried about the squatter. I want to push him more on this Ryan guy, see if I can get more information about him. It's pretty clear to me my husband thinks maybe the man just needed a place to stay, so he moved in for a bit.

Perhaps his wife left him.

Maybe he lost his house because he couldn't pay his mortgage.

There are a million reasons why someone might move out of their house and into a cabin in the middle of nowhere, and while I can think of an entire host of malicious reasons for someone to do that, the likelihood is that it's all innocent. Maybe this guy just needed a bit of time to get back on his feet after a rough patch.

We've all had those.

If I hadn't run into kind people who were willing to help me move to North Carolina, I don't know what I would have done. I certainly wouldn't be where I am in life, that much is for sure. I'd be — where, still stuck in my past? Perhaps worse — but it doesn't matter now.

What really matters is finding out who has been staying at the cabin. Finding out what they want. Figuring out how Ian and I can clean this place up, get it on the market. Start our family. Leave New York and never look back.

There's nothing here for him, and if you're to believe my husband when he's had a bit of wine, there really wasn't ever anything here for him. The hope of something, sure, maybe even the belief that he should try to stay connected to a place because that was where he was from, but nothing more than that.

Nothing concrete. Nothing tying us to New York except for this stupid cabin and the promise of a family once we get rid of it.

But that's not a problem for right now. That's a problem for later. What I need to worry about is how I can get the two of us out of this cabin as quickly as possible. Staring at the dressed deer in front of me isn't going to do any good. Wandering around outside instead of helping Ian get this place spruced up will only result in the two of us staying even longer than necessary.

Maybe, if we get this place cleaned up and ready to go on the market sooner than we thought, we can leave. We can spend the rest of our winter breaks curled up in bed together in North Carolina, as far away from this frozen hellscape as possible.

I know he doesn't want that, but I honestly think I can change his mind. If I show him how hard I've worked and tell him how much happier I'll be in North Carolina, then there's no reason why he won't be willing to head home with me.

That's what I'm going to do. He's working on fixing the power; I'll work on cleaning up the inside of the cabin.

Turning, I prepare myself to cut through the drifts back to the cabin. It's only now I realize just how cold I am and how grateful I'm going to be to get back in front of the fire. It's freezing out here, the wind cutting around the side of the cabin like a knife, slicing through my clothes and burning my skin.

I'm halfway back to the cabin when movement in the woods to my right catches my attention. I turn, my heart beating hard, only to see a flash of bright orange.

That's not a color you should find in the middle of a snowstorm. That's the color worn by hunters to ensure they're not gunned down by another maniac with a gun out in the woods.

It's gone before I can try to pinpoint where it is, but I know that color like I know my own name.

Someone is out there. And they're watching.

19

LIZZY

I killed my father when I was eighteen, shortly before I ran away from home and moved to Alabama, changed my name to Lizzy, started slinging burgers for a living, and was picked up off the side of the road by the man who ended up being just as dangerous as the one who knocked up my mother.

My mama said my father loved me, that some men show their love in a different way than we might want them to, but that doesn't mean they don't love us. The really messed-up thing about this entire situation with Zachary is that my mom would have been the perfect match for him.

She would have loved him changing her. She would have leaned into it, accepting all changes he made with open arms, not fighting them like I do. I know he's pleased with the way my nose looks, but I also know he's ready to do more to me.

He came into the bathroom last night after my shower and pulled my towel from me. I'm used to him poking my body, touching me even though I don't want him to, putting his hands on me, but it was different.

He had a marker with him.

Black lines appeared on my hips, my stomach, my breasts. I stood completely still, letting the felt tip of it slide over my skin, leaving behind proof of how ugly I am.

Of how ugly he thinks I am.

We were standing in front of the mirror, and while I didn't want to see what he was doing to me, he made me watch. Every time I closed my eyes, he grabbed my arm. Squeezed. Told me to open them.

"We'll take this in," he said, massaging my thigh. "Lift your breasts. Tuck your tummy." More lines appeared, most of them dotted, some solid, each a roadmap to the perfect body he wanted to give me.

I'd stood there, watching the lines appear. They were a dream to him, exactly what he wanted from me, but to me they were a nightmare. Every man I've ever spent more than some passing time with has wanted to change me. I had thought Zachary was different, that he really loved me.

But I was wrong. When I look at myself in the mirror, I don't see the beauty he claims he can turn me into. I see a tired version of me, someone who can barely stir up enough mental fortitude to get through the day. I thought ...

Well, what I thought was that I'd be able to kill Zachary. It should have been easy, to slit his throat or stab him or burn the house down, but he's careful. He makes his own drinks and handles his liquor better than most men.

He has all the knives in the kitchen locked in a cabinet when they're not in use. The only time I have access to them is when I'm cooking, and then he's there, hovering, watching. Waiting for me to try to slip one away, for me to force his hand for more punishment.

I know about the closet where he told me he'll happily lock me if I piss him off. I saw the handcuffs there on the wall, a silent promise of what he'd do to me to make sure I fell back in line. I can't treat this like a joke.

He certainly isn't.

I still have free rein of the house, but that's only because so far I haven't broken any of the rules he's made for me. I know perfectly well that if he were to find out what I think about when I'm lying under him in bed, he'd locked me up in the closet and throw away the key.

But my thoughts are private. I'm fully planning on killing him; that much is decided. The only problem is that I don't know how to do it. If I had access to a knife or a screwdriver or anything sharp and long and pointed. Knitting needles. An ice pick. I'd love to take one of those scalpels from downstairs that he showed me and shove it right through his eye.

Ahead of me, tucked in a corner of the room, the black eye of a camera stares at me. Not all of them are as obvious as this one. Without thinking about my actions or the consequences they may have, I lift my middle finger to it.

Feels good. It also makes me feel like a teenager desperate and grasping for any possible way of rebellion, of proving to their parents what terrible people they are. A single middle finger, raised in defiance. All I need now is an emo kid haircut and some pop-punk playing on my iPod and I'll be back in high school.

The thought makes cold sweat break out on the back of my neck. Anything dealing with high school, any thought of what it was like growing up in my parents' house makes me think of my father. But he's dead and gone. I saw to that.

Now the only man in my life who can ruin it all for me is my husband.

He's at work. Steam pours from the shower, and I get in, cringing away from the heat as it rushes over my body. It burns, my skin already turning red as it hits me, but I'm not getting out until the lines are gone. Sure, he'll draw them on again. He'll do it over and over until he's satisfied with the way I'm going to look; then he's calling in another favor, to get his doctor friend here again to assist him in the surgery he has planned.

But right now I want my body back.

Squeezing body wash onto my loofah, I run water over it, foam it up. Suds spill out over my hands, and I rub it up and down my body. Step under the spray to rinse it off.

The lines are still there. They're not as bold, not as accusatory, but I still see them. I scrub again, harder this time, sloughing off layers of skin in my effort to clean myself.

Back under the hot water.

Scrubbing again. Harder.

It takes me almost half the bottle of body wash, but in the end the black lines are a memory. I'm scrubbed clean, red from head to toe, my raw skin burning with the heat from the water. I get out, wrap myself in a fluffy white towel, and lie on my bed. At least I have creature comforts.

Ignoring the camera in the corner, I get up and dress, then walk downstairs. I've never been to his office at the hospital, of course, but if I close my eyes, I can picture him behind his computer, leaning forward, watching me. He'll have a patient's chart open just so he can tab over if necessary.

The great Dr. Zachary Pierce, everyone. A man so obsessed with perfection and ensuring that his life is the best it can be that he's willing to drive everyone he loves away from him and destroy the woman stupid enough to walk down the aisle to him. Abruptly I turn from the kitchen and walk into the living room. Pull the vacuum from the hall closet. Plug it in.

The floor is immaculate. He sees to that. It's one of my duties, and I make sure he never has reason to complain about how clean the house is. I vacuumed yesterday before he came home from work. I'm not looking for dirt right now.

I'm looking for something I could use to kill him.

There's the possibility of breaking a mirror and using a shard of it to stab him. Something poetic in that, in the fact that the one thing he used to check my perfection would be destroyed and used to destroy him. I file that thought away as I vacuum down the hall to his home office.

There's a camera facing the door, so I barely slow down as I walk past it, but I still reach out and give the doorknob a little twist.

Locked. As always.

Down the hall, then, to the formal dining room, which we only use when we have company. There are even fewer options for homemade weapons here. The chairs are all sturdy, with thick legs, so even if I could break one off, what would I do? Bludgeon him or stab him with it? He's not a vampire, after all.

The cord runs out. I turn off the vacuum, walk down the hall. Unplug it from the outlet and then plug it back in in the formal living room. From here it's a straight shot into the kitchen. I adjust the height of the vacuum to account for the tile and walk slowly around the massive island, the sound of the vacuum drowning out my footsteps.

This place is a chef's paradise, with everything I could ever need to whip up a five-star dining experience at the drop of a hat. The only thing missing are the knives, the spot where the knife block sits by the stove conspicuously empty. I let my eyes scan the room, taking in the hanging rack full of pots and pans, the stocked fridge, the magnets on it holding up a save-the-date for a nurse at the hospital.

He could swallow a few magnets. Bowel obstruction.

I could hit him over the head with a cast-iron pot.

Maybe I could poison him. Pausing by the sink, I open the cupboard under it, but the only things there are the trash can and some Windex. Nothing in the kitchen will help me kill my husband.

Slowly I leave the kitchen and walk into the living room. This is where the two of us eat, on either side of the table, squared off like opposing football teams. I try to look like I'm vacuuming, but really I'm paying attention to a framed award I've seen before but never really paid attention to.

It's in a shadowbox right behind where I sit, which is probably why I've noticed it but never really looked at it. From the Surgical Association of America, it was given to Dr. Zachary Pierce in honor of his commitment to improving the lives of the underprivileged.

It's not the certificate that gives me pause.

It's the scalpel in the middle of the shadowbox, mounted in place the way some people might mount a particularly large fish they catch.

I slow, vacuuming the same spot of carpet a few times, then bend over and adjust the height clearance of the machine. My back is to the camera, but I feel, more than ever, that Zachary is watching me. Keeping my head down, I try to look out of the corner of my eye at the scalpel.

I think it's a real one. It certainly looks real, with a blade designed to slice and save but could certainly be used to stab and kill instead. I want to take the box down, break the glass — *in case of emergency break this glass and save your life from your insane husband* — but he's watching me. I can practically feel his breath on the back of my neck as he leans closer to his computer screen, watching to see what I'm doing.

Watching to see if I'm really just vacuuming.

But maybe not. Maybe he's in surgery right now, saving some poor underprivileged person who will thank their lucky stars the great Dr. Pierce was at work today.

I stand. My heart beats hard, the throbbing of it in my chest almost enough to make me sick.

He might not be watching. There's no way for me to know

for sure, not without asking him, and that would be a death sentence in itself.

But then there's the crackle of a speaker, and my husband's voice fills the room, putting to bed any question I had of whether or not he knew what I was doing.

20

BETH

I close the cabin door and lean against it, breathing heavily, my head pounding. "Shit," I mutter, then strip my gloves, dropping them to the floor. They're wool and handmade. I bought them at a mountain craft fair last year, and while they're doing a great job keeping my hands warm, I can't stand the feeling of the wool on my skin right now.

"Oh, God, someone is out there." Turning back, I open the door just a crack and peer through. There's so much pressure in my head it feels like my skull is going to crack, and I'm craving a drink to take the edge off, but I can't do that right now, can't walk away from this door without trying to make sure Ian is okay.

Nothing moves. Yes, some snow swirls across the ground, blown by the wind like sand on the beach. It drifts up against the shed, creating huge fluffy piles of snow that glitter like diamonds and look soft like frosting.

I close the door. Pause a moment. Throw the bolt.

Then I'm off like a shot, running through the cabin to the back bedroom, climbing up on the huge four-poster bed and peering out the window into the backyard. I look for any flash of orange, hoping against hope that there won't be anything there. If someone is out there with Ian, I don't know what I'm going to do.

No orange. Just white. Brown. Then navy blue moves along the side of the house, just barely in my field of vision. I have to turn my head all the way to the right and press my face against the freezing glass to see what's happening. Ian stands, brushing his hands together, then plants them on his hips. He leans forward, his hands out of sight, so I can't see what he's doing.

A low hum runs through the cabin.

I watch his face split into a smile; then he turns and starts walking to the side of the cabin. Hurrying to meet him, I jump off the bed and run into the living room, only pausing long enough to look up at the light when I realize it's on.

It casts a warm glow around the cabin. Mya jumps down from the sofa and walks over to me, purring as she does. She twines between my legs, and I pick her up, holding her to my chest.

"He did it, darling. Can you believe it?" I mutter the words into her warm fur, then carry her with me to the front door. It rattles in its frame; then there's a hard knock on the wood.

"Beth, I'm half-frozen to death out here, and if you don't let me in soon, then I'm not sure if I'll be able to have kids at all or if it will shrivel up and fall off!" He's laughing, and I almost feel like laughing, too, but then I remember why I locked the door, and I put Mya down.

Throw the bolt. Open the door. Reach through and pull Ian in by his scarf. Glance outside. Slam the door. Bolt it again.

Ian's grinning at me as he unwinds his scarf, but his smile melts from his face. "What in the world is wrong, Beth? Are you okay? Why did you have the door locked?"

"Someone's out there." I point at the door accusatorially like we'll be able to see through it to whoever has been walking around the cabin. "I saw them, Ian. I saw them hovering at the edge of the woods. Watching."

"You saw them?" He stops unwinding, a frown on his face. "Who was it?"

Who was it? "I don't know, Ian. They were wearing orange and skulking around the edge of the woods. Watching."

"Skulking?" He laughs and finally resumes unwinding his scarf, dropping it to the floor when it's off.

I bend without thinking and pick it up. If it stays in a pile on the floor, then it'll be cold and damp when he wants to put it back on.

I catch myself and shake my head. That kind of thinking is what I had to do before, not now. Still, old habits die hard.

He unzips his coat. "Wait, and they were wearing orange?"

I nod.

"Well, then it's just a hunter. He probably was trying to track the deer we found yesterday. Did you call out to him?"

I stare at Ian, trying to tell if he's joking or not, but the expression on his face tells me he's quite serious and thinks I should have called out to whoever was watching me.

"I didn't," I say, speaking slowly. "I was scared, and he turned and then disappeared. Even if I had called out, I don't know if he would have heard me."

Ian shrugs. This is easy for him, and I feel anger rise in me.

If I were as innocent as Ian, as sheltered and protected, then maybe I'd also be able to shrug this off as no big deal. But I can't, and the fact that he's insistent on seeing everything as perfectly fine is enough to make me feel like I'm going crazy.

"Ian, I don't understand what's going on right now, and I know you're not worried, but I need you to take this seriously.

Someone was living here without your knowledge or permis-
sion, and then there was the deer, the cat, the hunter ..." I'm
ticking things off on my fingers to try to really drive my point
home. "You don't think something weird is going on here?"

"Beth, listen to me." He's hung his coat on a hook by the
door and takes his scarf from me to hang it up as well. "This
is where I grew up. Things are different here. When someone
is cold, they find a place to sleep. When they need food, they
might take something from your outside larder if you have
one. I'm not worried about someone taking what they need to
survive when I'm not here to use it. Do you understand?"

"But the person —"

"Is probably hungry. And cold. Whoever was here, in our
cabin, needed to be here. I'm glad we could offer them a little
shelter from the storm. They'll come back, pick up Mya, grab
whatever else they may have left, and then be on their way.
I'm not going to begrudge someone who needs something."

God, my husband is a better person than I am. I stare at him,
trying to wrap my mind around how the two of us ended up
together when it's clear he's kinder, smarter, and more loving.

I just got lucky, I guess.

"Now, are you going to stand here worried about who
might be outside, or are you going to tell me what a good job
I did getting the lights turned back on in here?"

"You are incredible." I kiss him, leaning against him as he
wraps his arms around me. He wants more from me, I know
that he does, but right now all I want is to let him hold me so
I can try to calm down. There's a small part of me trying to
believe that he's right, that whoever is here — Ryan, apparently, according to Ian — doesn't want anything other than a
nice warm place to rest his head. I want to believe that.

I do. I really do. But I don't.

"Now, sweet wife, why don't we see if there's anything in

the bedroom that needs our attention?" He murmurs the words into my neck.

Goosebumps break out all over my skin, and I shiver, breathing in deep to smell his cologne.

"I think the bedroom is all clean and ready for us to sell the cabin." I giggle a little, knowing my reticence is going to drive him crazy.

"Well, there's no shame in messing it up a little bit." He forks his fingers through my hair and leans in like he's going to kiss me. "You trust me, right, Beth?"

"Of course I trust you." Looping my arms around his neck, I lean away from him a bit so I can get a better look at him. Ian is so handsome. That, along with how kind he was to me when I accidentally spilled my drink on him when we first met, drew me to him. I love just staring at my husband, and sometimes I have no idea how I got so lucky. "If I didn't believe you, would I do this?"

I trace my finger down his jaw, and I'm about to kiss him again when he pulls away from me.

"Did you hear that?"

"Nope." I don't hear much of anything but the wind howling around the cabin, and now that he's put romantic thoughts in my mind as well as calmed me down some, I'm not interested in talking about what he thinks he heard. "Don't hear anything. You said not to worry about it."

He grabs my hands, holding them out in between our bodies. "I'm serious, Beth. I think I heard someone calling."

I freeze. Whatever warmth there was in my body a moment ago is suddenly gone, and I shiver, leaning up against him to try to steal some of his. The fire is still crackling and burning in the fireplace, but it doesn't cross my mind to move closer to it. I'm paying too much attention to the expression on his face.

His brow is furrowed, his mouth pinched into a straight line.

"Ian?" My voice shakes a little.

"Shh. Listen." He puts a finger up against my lips.

Nothing. I hear nothing. It's like when you press a shell up against your ear after going on vacation to the beach in the hopes that you'll be able to capture some of the sound of the waves, but there's nothing there but your own blood whooshing through your veins and arteries, your own life force making music in your ear.

"Someone's outside."

Right on cue, as if we were in a play and someone is perfectly following their lines, there's the sound of footsteps on the porch. I hear stamping, like whoever is out there is trying to get the snow off their boots.

Then silence.

Someone tries the doorknob. It rattles.

I can't move. I'm no longer cold, but I feel frozen to the spot, completely unable to move. Ian shivers, turns. He takes a step towards the door. My fingers pluck at his shirt, sliding from the fabric. I can't stop him.

God help me, I don't know what's happening, but I can't stop any of it. Fear creeps up the back of my neck like cold fingers, and I shiver.

I don't want Ian to open that door.

There's hammering at the door.

"Hello? I think you accidentally locked me out! Can you let me in, please?"

"Ian, no." I whisper the words, hoping my husband hears them, but like a man drawn to the Siren's call, he's already crossing the room to the front door, his hand outstretched to open it.

21

LIZZY

"Lizzy, I promise you if you try to hurt me with that scalpel, I will lock you in the basement, and you'll never see the light of day again. What do you think about that?"

I freeze, my hand still outstretched, my eyes locked on the scalpel. It seemed like such a good idea, like the only way I could actually find any peace living in this house, but now that he knows what I was thinking, it's all over.

"Go downstairs." The speaker crackles again.

I turn around, willing my heart to slow down. My eyes flick up to the camera. How did I get so unlucky as to try to do something to save myself right when Zachary is watching? It's the worst possible timing.

"Downstairs?" I force the word.

"Downstairs. Now. I'm going to lock the basement door when you're where you're supposed to be. You're going somewhere safe so I don't have to worry about you doing anything stupid until I get home. Do it, Lizzy. Right now. Don't make me come home early."

I shiver and turn away from the camera. Even as I start

walking towards the basement door, I hate myself for it. I should fight back. I should scream at him, dare him to come home and make me go to the basement. But my feet are traitors, and I'm standing at the top of the basement stairs before I realize that I'm actually going to do what he just told me to.

But can he really lock me in? I know he's taken steps to turn this place into my own personal prison. The doors and windows are impenetrable, but maybe he was bluffing about locking the door. Maybe — and then I look closer at the knob and see the little box there, the one that connects to the rest of the house's smart system, and I know he was telling the truth.

Closing the door behind me, I stand at the top of the stairs. My heart beats in my ears, but I still hear the mechanic sound of the door lock sliding into place. Without thinking, I turn and try the handle.

It doesn't budge.

"Make yourself at home, Lizzy. You have ten seconds."

Again his voice fills the air. I look up, searching for the speaker. It must be coming from the camera downstairs.

"Ten. Nine."

"Ten seconds until what?" I start down the stairs, one hand on the railing to ensure I don't fall.

"Six. Five."

"Until what?" At the bottom now, I scream the words into the room. I'd been able to keep the fear at bay, convince myself that I could handle whatever it was Zachary was going to do to me. But it's the fear of the unknown that terrifies me.

"Two. One."

The lights shut out. I stumble forward, my hands outstretched, my fingers searching for anything that will help me find where I am.

"Feel free to nap until I get home. Then we'll talk about your punishment."

There's a loud click, and I look up, my eyes already adjusting to the dark.

I remember there's a camera in here. I just don't remember where exactly it is. He might still be watching, or he might have disappeared.

Maybe he got called away to perform lifesaving surgery.

A sob escapes me. Wouldn't that just be rich? The town's most popular doctor, the one we were all so lucky to have move here to bless us with his talents, the one nobody could understand why he'd come because he's just *that talented*, locks his wife in the basement and turns out the light before going and taking care of a patient. Look at him go, people, look at how skillfully he saves one life while ruining another.

I collapse. The floor is hard and cold, and pain shoots through me when my knees collide with it. Falling forward on my hands, I start to crawl towards the bed. I don't want to be on it, don't want to try to find any comfort in anything Zachary has given me, but I'm exposed.

I'm terrified.

And I'm pissed.

I reach the bed and pull myself up, rubbing my knees as I turn and sit on the edge. I'd thought I could make out some shapes before, when the lights first went off, but I know now how wrong I was. It was wishful thinking. The basement is pitch black, the type of dark that most people rarely experience.

Usually there's some sort of light — manmade or natural — but I can't see a thing right now.

"Dammit, Zachary!" I stand, my hand grasping for something I can use to throw at the camera. Who knows if he's watching? Without any light to tell me the camera's on or a sound to clue me in, I have no idea. So many people think cameras have red blinking lights. They don't. They're just black eyes, watching, a window into my world he can easily slip through. Does it really matter? He can always play back the footage later if he wants to watch me have an absolute meltdown. The tray covered with instruments is gone. I know now that was only here to shock me and show me what I was going to have to live through at his hands.

He wasn't ever going to leave it down here where I might be able to get my hands on it.

There's nothing down here I can use as a weapon, nothing that will save me from my husband when he gets home. Still, I grope through the dark, well aware that he could be sitting in his office right now, watching me on his phone's screen, laughing at the way I'm crouched over, at how I'm fumbling around like an idiot.

Rage burns in me. I've thought it before — that I need to kill him, just like I killed my father. But thinking it and going through with it are two totally different things. He's always one step ahead of me, always able to figure out how to keep me in this house without any chance of getting out.

And then, the one time I think I might be able to take my life back, he's paying attention.

How the hell am I going to escape if he's watching me every moment of every day? And how in the world did he know what I was doing? There's no way he has time to just sit around and watch the cameras to see what I'm doing. I can see him checking in from time to time, sure, wanting to know what hell he's put me through, but to jump on it like that?

I freeze, my mind racing. I can't seem to move my body while my mind tears through thoughts like this. I need time to focus on each one as I try to figure out what I'm going to do.

"He knows what I'm doing the moment I do it," I say, whispering the words to myself. It's comforting to me to hear my voice in the silence of the basement. I'm turned away from the camera, my chin dropped down to my chest. There's very little chance, if any, that Zachary can hear me through the camera.

Still, the words come out in a whisper. More of a breath than anything.

"How does he know what I'm doing right when I do it?"

I close my eyes. Think. The entire house is automated. With the touch of a button he can lock doors, turn off lights, watch what I'm doing.

It hits me, and I have to bite down on my tongue to keep from screaming. He has to have motion sensors installed in the house. I wouldn't be surprised if he gets a notification when I move from one camera zone to another. I can just see the little message popping up on his phone screen, the greedy look on his face as he taps it, the way he licks his lips as he stares at me to try to figure out what I'm doing.

So he always knows what I'm doing.

Now that I know that, what good will it do me?

I walk back to the bed and sit down. The mattress is firm, and I grip the edge of it with both hands like holding onto it will ground me. I want something solid and supportive in my life right now, and this stupid mattress is the only thing I have.

If he's getting a notification every time I move from room to room, then I can do one of two things. I can try to throw him off the case of what I'm really doing by moving quickly from room to room.

Or I can take my time. Spend a lot of time in one room. Daydream about how I'm going to kill him and what I need to do it. I've walked through the house enough that I have the rooms practically memorized. It shouldn't be a big deal for me to sit and think about what weapons I might have at my disposal — or what weapons I can make.

And then he won't know what I'm doing. If I'm in one

room plotting how to kill him with something from another, then maybe he'll never see it coming.

I close my eyes. Take a deep breath. Relaxing feels impossible, but I still try. There's no telling how long he's going to keep me down here.

22

BETH

The man on the front porch bursts into the living room of the cabin, bringing with him a fresh shower of snow that falls on the floor, the smell of cold air, and a grin so wide it almost looks fake.

I hang back, watching the scene as it plays out in front of me, almost afraid to draw attention to myself by walking up and shaking the man's hand. Of course, he knows I'm here. I saw how he looked around the room as if taking stock of what was there and what wasn't. I'm here, standing behind Ian, and his eyes landed on me for a moment before bouncing off.

"Ryan McKinney," he says, thrusting a huge hand out to my husband. "I pop in from time to time to take care of the cabin. And you are?"

"Ian Myers," Ian replies, shaking the man's hand. Actually, it's more like a paw, what the stranger has attached to his arm. His hand completely engulfs my husband's, and I know Ian notices it in the way he glances down at where the two of them are touching. "I'm the owner, here to clean the place up and get it on the market. It's so nice to finally meet you face-to-face." There's a slight pause, and I can't help the feeling that the two of them are sizing each other up — for what, I don't know. But just like animals will size each other up in the wild, my husband and the stranger seem to be doing the same thing. "And this is my lovely wife, Beth."

"Beth." The stranger — no, not an unknown stranger, *Ryan*, just like Ian told me from the beginning — silently moves past Ian and takes my hand in his. I didn't even realize I'd offered it for him to shake before it was enveloped in his maw.

No, his paw.

"It's a pleasure," I say, tucking my hands into the pockets of my jeans. "Ian has told me a lot about how kind you are to keep this place running smoothly and how much work that has to be. He was really lucky to find you."

"Oh, I was the lucky one. Me and the cat." He glances over my shoulder at Mya.

Mya, who usually comes to wind around my legs whenever she has a chance, now stands on the back of the sofa, her back slightly arched, her golden eyes locked on Ryan.

"She seems angry with you," I offer.

"I'd say. She's a bit upset I left her last night to do some hunting. Got caught out in that storm, hunkered down in a cave a bit away. You probably know it." He turns to Ian, who shrugs, then continues as if my husband agreed with him. "Yep, not too far from here. It's rough, but it kept the snow off me for the most part. Then I come up here and find I'm locked out." He chuckles.

Ian laughs, too. I don't.

Do I know this man? If pressed, I'd say that I'd never seen him before in my life, but there's something about him that feels familiar. Not his size, a man like this is a mountain, someone you'd remember passing on the street or accidentally brushing against in a bar. It's his eyes, I think, the cruel cast they have even though he's smiling as he speaks.

"Out all night in this storm?" Ian, ever the consummate gentleman, clears his throat. "You have to be about frozen. Let's get some coffee going and see if you can warm up. Did you not get my email that we were coming up this weekend to clean out the house?"

Ryan shakes his head. Turns from me to speak to Ian. I immediately relax. Just having his gaze off me is enough to make me feel like I can breathe again.

"I can't say I did. I'm sorry."

"Really? I would have sworn you responded and said that was fine." Ian's voice is light, unbothered. It's the same tone I've heard him take with students he's run into outside of school who haven't done all of their assignments. It means *you think you're getting one over on me, but I'm a hell of a lot smarter than I look, young man.*

And Ryan must pick up on it.

"You know what?" He smacks his palm against his forehead and lets out a low groan. "I think I do remember that now. I just got all my dates confused and thought I'd get up here to bag a deer for the missus. She's pregnant, again, and craving venison. Isn't that just the strangest thing you've ever heard?"

I watch Ian's shoulders relax. His back is to me as he gets coffee for Ryan, but I can see how relieved he is by what Ryan just said. Malicious intent is one thing, but getting venison for a pregnant wife and spacing out on the date we'd be here? That's another completely.

"That's all right," Ian says, turning around with two steaming mugs of coffee. He hands one to Ryan and gestures for me to come take the other. I do; then he pours a third and sits down at the table. I sit next to him, Ryan across from me.

Why do I feel like the two of us are on trial?

"So tell me again why you want to sell the old place?" Ryan takes a sip of his coffee, his eyes locked on Ian's face.

I go to follow suit, but the brew is so hot it singes the tip of my tongue. Contenting myself with just holding the mug for warmth, I turn to my husband.

"We want to start a family." Ian pauses, and I wonder how much he's going to tell this guy. He shares everything on social media, so all Ryan would have to do was look him up and learn all about our struggles. Infertility. Paying for IVF. Even when Ian married me, I knew I wasn't going to have an easy time getting pregnant.

I didn't before.

Thank God.

"Babies are expensive." Ryan nods. Takes another sip. My taste buds cry out in pain just watching him drink his coffee. "I hate to pry, but things must not be going well if you need a chunk of change like what this place will get you."

"We're looking into IVF," I offer, wanting Ian to know I'm here and supporting him in this conversation. I reach out, take his hand. Squeeze it. "It's expensive, and we don't get up here to use this place anyway."

"You can't have kids?" Ryan turns his gaze on me. I see it again — cruelty there, masked by something to try to hide it — but it's gone before I can really pay attention to it. "I'm sorry to hear that. You've always had problems?"

"This is the first time I've ever tried," I lie. "You think things will be easy, so it's a surprise when it isn't."

"Isn't that just the piss of it?" Ryan drains his mug. Walks to the kitchen and refills it. Sits back down. Mine is still untouched, as is Ian's. "You never know what's going to come your way."

We're all silent. I wonder if Ian is having the same thoughts I am, about how to get this guy out of the cabin.

Mya wanders over, jumps into my lap. I pet her, noticing how she turns her gaze on Ryan but doesn't go to him.

"Well, I can't thank you enough for all of the work you've done keeping this place up and running." Ian stands, stretches. I've seen him do this move a thousand times when he's trying to get someone to leave our house. He makes it so the visitors feel like they're doing us a favor by leaving so we can get some rest.

That's what will happen here. Ryan will leave, the two of us will laugh about it, and then we'll be on our merry way. Now that the electricity is fixed, I hope we can be out of here in two days, tops. Maybe three if we uncover any major problems.

"Oh, it's been my pleasure. Thanks for understanding what I was doing here even though you were coming back. And for dressing my deer."

"Oh, you were the one in the orange," I say, finally putting two and two together.

Both men turn to look at me.

"I'm sorry, I thought I saw someone in a hunting vest outside and got a little creeped out. But it was just you."

"Just me." He smiles. It doesn't look natural on his face.

"I'll give you the venison I took off the deer, no problem." Ian's still standing. "It's in a cooler I found out in the shed. Hey, you can even take the cooler with you, what do you say about that? I'll finish skinning the deer later. Why don't I show you where it is, and you can be on your way before it gets dark? I have no doubt your wife would love to have you home sooner rather than later."

So it wasn't Ian who skinned the deer. I'd been afraid of that, but hearing him say he didn't finish only makes me more nervous.

"Oh, I think I'll stay a while." He drains half of his mug, puts it on the table. "I'm not in a rush to get out of here. Last night was cold out there in the cave, and I'd prefer to warm up a bit longer."

"Stay as long as you'd like," Ian tells him, ignoring the dark look I shoot him. "But we definitely don't want you to be home too late to your wife. I'm sure she'll miss you."

"She might." Ryan stands. He towers over Ian, and I see the way my husband looks up at him. "Thanks for the coffee. I think I'll take a little nap now. It's damn near impossible to get a good night's sleep out there in a roaring storm when it feels like your fingers and your pecker will freeze right off."

He leaves the table, his mug still where he was sitting, and strolls to the bedroom, pausing only long enough to throw another log on the fire. Sparks fly into the air, but he ignores them and shuts the door behind him.

I shiver when I hear him lock it.

"Ian?" I ask, finally turning to look at my husband. His face is pale, his eyes wide. "Ian, what the hell was that? Why does he think he can just move in like that?"

He doesn't respond.

"You need to get that man out of the cabin." My voice is tight. I'm whispering so Ryan can't hear me. Mya gets agitated with me and hops off my lap, meowing her complaints. She walks to the sofa and silently jumps up before curling into a little donut. "Ian, what does he want?"

"I have no idea." My husband sounds genuinely confused. He's staring at the closed bedroom door like answers are going to appear on the wood in big bold letters for us to figure out what the hell is going on. "Beth, I'm sorry, but I have no clue what's going on here."

I don't, either. I want to tell Ian I don't trust Ryan, that there's something about him that scares me, that we need to kick him out, but it won't do any good, and I already know that.

We both know we need to get this man out of the cabin. Neither one of us knows how to do that.

I just wonder if Ian feels the same fear that I do.

He probably doesn't. I'm the only one who has a reason to.

23

LIZZY

"You were thinking of doing something stupid today." Zachary stares at me from across the table. While he watched this evening, I pulled leftovers out of the refrigerator and made quesadillas. He has a margarita, but I'm drinking ice water. I wouldn't have wanted alcohol, but he didn't offer it to me anyway.

He's trying to punish me, and while that would have upset me before, I'm over it. He can do whatever he wants to me, but I'm getting out of here. I'm locking myself in my mind and focusing on what I have to do to survive. He can't get in my head, and that's the one thing I keep hanging on to.

He doesn't know what I'm thinking.

"I hadn't really looked at that award before." My voice is bland — it's not as if this is completely untrue — and he glances up sharply at me. Of course he knows it's not the whole truth. He's not stupid. If he were, he never would have been able to get away with what he's done to me so far. He's clever and conniving, but I need to be one step ahead of him.

"Right. It just so happens that award has a scalpel in it." He gestures to the empty spot above my head. "And I had to put it away. Thanks for taking away the one thing I liked to look at during meals." Something in me wonders why he has left it out this long, with a sharp blade inside just for the taking.

He's not going to get to me. I'm not hungry, and every bite makes me want to throw up, but I force myself to eat. I need my strength to not only come up with a plan of how to get out of here, but also to go through with it. As much as I'd like to just go to bed and fall asleep, I need to be smarter than him.

We're down to the wire now. I can feel it.

"Maybe if you were prettier, though, I wouldn't want to throw up when I look at you." He stares at me, then takes a long drink of his margarita. I rimmed it with salt, just the way he likes it, and he's worked his way around the glass, licking and sucking it off.

I stare at him for a moment, waiting for him to continue.

"That's why I want to go ahead and get you more surgery. Remember, darling, if it's worth doing, it's worth doing right, and I'm going to make sure you're perfect. Men will want you, and women will want to be you, although I think they already do. They envy you, you know that?" He leans forward, reaching across the table for me.

I don't move. Even though I want to pull back from him, I'm afraid that would set him off.

He continues when I don't answer. "I know women want me. How does that make you feel, that you're the one I chose?"

I swallow. My fork is in my hand, and without thinking, I suddenly stand, stabbing it down into his palm. The tines sink through his flesh and hit the wood of the table underneath.

Zachary stands, bellowing, his face turning a bright shade of red. His eyes are wide, and he stares at the fork before looking up at me.

"I'll kill you!"

I shake my head to clear the vision. It was only a vision. Of course I wouldn't risk stabbing him with a fork, something he could easily pull out and come after me in retaliation.

My fork trembles in my hand, and I put it down, resting it on the edge of the plate. "I feel great," I tell him. *Great because I'm the only person brave enough to kill you.*

"Lucky girl. Have you decided what surgery you want next?"

This is a trick question. I need to guess the thing that he wants me to change about myself, or he's going to get angry with me. If I choose the wrong thing to fix, then he'll blow up at me, and I'll have to deal with him telling me how fat, ugly, *and* stupid I am. A girl can only take so much.

"My stomach." I've seen the way he looks at me when I'm getting dressed. His eyes flick to my stomach, which was perfectly flat when we got married, and his eyes narrow. He hates it. I know he does.

"Good choice." Another sip of his margarita. "It's a bit more involved than your nose, but there's more work to be done. I'll get it booked in the next week or so, have my friend come back down to help me out."

That's how long I have to be free from this madman. If there were any way to get in contact with someone who might help me, I'd do it. I'd risk telling someone everything about what's going on, even in front of Zachary, if it meant I could get out of here. But he'll never let that happen. There's no way in hell he's going to let me have time around anyone right now, not when he's planning another surgery.

He may be a psycho, but he's smart.

"I'll fix you. Make sure you're no longer ugly. What do you say about that?"

There's a current of danger in his voice. I hear it and know I need to heed the warning.

"I can't thank you enough." The words are sand in my mouth. They're uncomfortable to speak, and I take a long sip of my water to wash the taste away. Screw it, I might as well lay it on thick if I'm going to try to get out of here soon. I know he doesn't trust me, but I can try to make him think I'm not a danger to him. "Seriously, Zachary, what you're doing for me is so kind. I can tell how much you love me."

He's silent for a moment, and I'm afraid I went too far. I have to remind myself that my husband is brilliant, and he can easily see through my lies, but then he breaks into a smile. We're either both lying now, both of us trying to hide our true selves from the person across the table, or he's falling for what I'm saying.

I glance at his drink. It's empty.

"It's really nice to finally be appreciated around here. You know, I work so hard, long hours all day, and when I come home, I just want to be thanked." He stands, bracing his hand on the table for support. I notice how wobbly he is on his feet.

He's always so careful.

Maybe now's the time. Maybe I should rush him, knock him over, try to get out of here tonight. Even if I don't kill him — which is what I want to do more than anything in my life right now — I can escape. Go to the police. Get a restraining order. I can get away from him, and shouldn't that be enough?

No. It's not enough, and it wouldn't ever be enough. The only thing that will give me peace about this time in my life is knowing that Zachary is dead. And that he suffered.

That I made him suffer.

"Well, I appreciate you." I stand to start clearing dishes from the table. "Seriously, Zachary, it took me a while to come to grips with it, but I know you love me. You're doing this because you love me. I just didn't see it and couldn't see it, not when I had such a terrible relationship with my father."

"He was terrible to you, wasn't he, Lizzy?"

Zachary's words surprise me so much I turn to look at him. Does he really care? For a moment, it almost sounded like he cared about me, but I know that's not true. He cares about using me, manipulating me. But he doesn't care about who I am as a person.

"Yes."

"And that's why you had to kill him."

I nod. "Yes."

"But I'm not terrible to you."

I don't like this conversation. I don't like the fact that he seems to be having the same thought process I am. He has to know I hate him and that I've thought about hurting him before, but if he's thinking about me killing him, or thinks for a moment that I might, then I'm in trouble.

"No, you're amazing." I put the plate I'm holding down and walk around the table to him. It makes me want to be sick, but I wrap my arms around him and lean my head against his chest. I can hear his heart, so sturdy and reliable, the two things I thought he was when we first met. Revulsion rises in me when he reaches up and twines his fingers through my hair.

"I want you to remember that." His voice changes. Gone is the wistful tone it had a moment ago. The danger is back. Anger, electric with power and desire, runs through his words. I try to pull away from him, but he's fisted his hand into my hair now and holds me in place so I can't move. "I want you to remember that I'm amazing, Lizzy. Remember where you came from and what I've done for you."

"I remember." The words come out in a squeak. He's pulling my hair so hard now that my scalp burns. I imagine him plucking every hair out of my head just to punish me for lying to him. He'd do it. I know he would.

"Remember that I'm good to you. I'm better than anyone has ever been to you. I don't hurt you like your father did, Lizzy. I love you and want to make you perfect so you deserve to be with me."

"I know." My cheek is flat against his chest just to keep the pain in my scalp at bay. Tears spring to my eyes, but I don't move to wipe them away. Let them fall. Let them soak into his shirt. Maybe he might have a moment of clarity then and realize what a monster he really is, but I don't think so.

If anything, he'd enjoy knowing I was crying.

"If you even think about hurting me again, I will kill you. I'll make it look like an accident, don't think I won't. You might have learned how to kill someone thanks to your dear old dad, but I learned a hell of a lot from mine, too." He laughs. The sound is hollow and echoes in my ear.

"I wouldn't hurt you."

He yanks my hair so suddenly, so hard, that I yelp. I was standing, leaning on him, but now I'm on the floor, massaging the back of my scalp. The tears that were brimming in my eyes now flow freely down my cheeks, and I hate looking up at him from this position, but I do anyway, more to see what he might do to me than anything else.

"No, you wouldn't. You *couldn't*. You're too stupid, Lizzy, too slow. But I'm watching you all the time, remember that. I see everything. I know what you're doing, and I'm *in — your — head*." He stabs his finger into the center of my forehead three times to punctuate the words.

I don't blink.

"I will break you and remake you. Why fight it?"

There's no answer I can give him, so I just stare at him. My knees ache from falling on them, but I'm not moving while he stands over me like this. Any movement might be seen as an act of aggression, and he'll hurt me. I know he will. He's done it before.

"You're nothing. I'll make you into something, Lizzy, just like my dear old dad did for my mom. He loved her enough to make her perfect, just like I love you, so you'd better like it. Next week the fat you're carrying around is gone." He sniffs and gives a little nod. "Now, clean this up. I'll be watching, so don't try anything stupid. I've had a long day, and I want you in my bed in twenty minutes."

I stand, shaking. He might think the way I'm shivering is due to fear, but I'm angry, really angry.

I could break a plate and stab him with the pieces, but he's standing over me. He's stronger than I am. I can't take the fork and ram it into the side of his neck. He's careful, always one step ahead of me, and seems to know what I'm thinking.

But I've killed to save myself once before.

And I won't have a problem doing it again.

24

BETH

Ryan doesn't emerge from the bedroom until later in the afternoon. Ian and I, instead of working around the cabin so we can clean it up, have sat on the sofa together, books in our laps, lost in our own thoughts.

From time to time I'd lean over to whisper something to him, my eyes on the bedroom door, wondering what the man locked inside it really wants with us. Ian wouldn't whisper back, almost as if he thought any form of communication would be enough to rouse Ryan from his nap and make him come out to see what we were talking about.

Finally the door swings open, groaning on its hinges, and I look up in surprise. Ryan runs a hand through his hair — no, *across* his hair. It's cut short, like a flat top, a high and tight, something military or police — and I speak before taking time to fully form what I'm going to say.

"You're police? Or military?"

He looks surprised. "Army. Ex-army."

"Why are you out?"

A slight pause. "I'm just no longer in."

There's something hidden there, something he wants to keep from the two of us — now that I know he has a secret, I'm determined to uncover it. Ian, bless his heart, is oblivious to everything going on between this intruder and me. I can feel the tension in the air, so thick it's choking, but Ian stands, putting his book down on the sofa.

"I'm going to get some wood for the fire. Why don't you figure out if you want to take food with you for your return trip home, and Beth will pack it up for you?" He waits for acknowledgment.

Ryan nods.

It seems as if Ian thinks he can simply ignore the problem in front of the two of us and it will go away. I want to scream at him that I need him to handle this and get Ryan out of the house, but that's not who my husband is. It's the first time he's being tested, and he's crumpling under the pressure instead of rising to the challenge.

"Great." Ian rubs his hands together. "Beth, do you mind making Ryan something to eat? I'm sure he's hungry and probably has a bit of a hike to his car."

"Snowmobile," Ryan corrects. "I'll just snowmobile out of here when it's time for me to go."

We all pause. I don't know what my husband is thinking, but I'm wondering why Ryan can't leave now if he has a snowmobile here and could easily get out of our hair. My husband must have forgotten the snowmobile and how he offered to let Ryan take our cooler.

He's not thinking straight.

I want to scream at him for bringing all of this on the two of us, but really, it's not his fault. You can't control what other people will do, only your own actions.

I mean, what did I expect, for Ian to fly up here every month or so to make sure the place was in good condition?

That would be utterly insane, but if he had done that, then there wouldn't be any conflict in the cabin right now. I can't seem to shake the feeling that Ryan knows something he shouldn't, or that there's another shoe about to drop, and I don't know what it is.

He's creepy, that much is obvious. But there's more to it than that. I'm sure of it.

"I'm happy to make you something to eat," I say, sounding more on autopilot than anything. Our cooler we brought from the car is still in the kitchen, loaded down with ice to keep everything cool. In retrospect, we could have easily just put everything out on the porch in the snow, and it would have kept just fine.

Still, I wasn't comfortable keeping food outside where something could easily come along and eat it. No sense in tempting the wildlife — foxes or bears or who knows what. I move slowly, pulling out sliced ham and cheese and making Ryan a sandwich. I thought I was hungry, but the thought of eating anything right now is enough to turn my stomach. Until I know what this guy wants — no, scratch that. Until he's gone and Ian and I are gone and back home where the two of us belong, in North Carolina, far away from upstate New York and this little cabin — I don't think I'm going to be able to fully relax.

Ryan takes the plate from me with a smile. "This looks great, Beth. Thanks for making it."

"My pleasure." I turn to the door, looking for Ian. He's not back yet, which shouldn't bother me, not really. The snow is deep, and it will take him a few minutes to reach the wood-pile, gather some logs, and carry them back. Still, I don't like being left alone with Ryan. I don't know what it is about him, but he seems familiar.

Of course, that's silly. I'd remember if I'd run into him

before. There's something about him — some sharp knife-edge of attitude in the way he looks at me and how he moves — that gives me pause. Surely I'd remember someone like him, who oozed danger and looked at me like he couldn't decide if he would rather smile at me or destroy me.

Yes, I've met a lot of people in my life. Some of them were definitely more dangerous than others, but I have no clear reason to be afraid of his guy. Ian vetted him, apparently. He trusts him with a key to the cabin and doesn't seem really worried that the man is still here and not in an obvious hurry to leave.

So why do I feel so uncomfortable?

Perhaps it's because of the casual way Ryan said he'd been in the army but now wasn't and how he skipped over the reason why he's no longer military. I don't like people who seem to have secrets.

Which is ironic, I know. If I based all trust and interactions off of whether or not I thought someone was always telling the truth when I spoke to them, then there wouldn't be any way I could look in the mirror.

"So. The military." I'm floundering for any idea of what to say next, and if he notices that I'm struggling, he doesn't seem to care. He's certainly not going to help me out by filling the silence, that much is obvious. "What made you decide to join?"

I cringe. There are dozens of reasons why someone would want to join the army. Maybe he wanted to grow up to be just like his father or grandfather. Maybe he didn't have money for college.

Or the aptitude for college.

Looking at him, I'm not sure that's the problem. There's a deep intelligence there behind his eyes, something that tells me this man is really smart. He might be more inclined to

using his muscles rather than his brains, but I have a feeling
—

"I was interested in the skills it could provide me." He chews
his sandwich mechanically. I wonder if he's even tasting it.

"Skills? Like what? You're big into guns?" I'm nervous but
interested, and I perch on the arm of the sofa. I don't want to
get too close to him, but I also don't want him to think I'm
shying away from him.

"Guns, sure. I like guns." He remains silent as he inhales
his sandwich, and I don't interrupt his eating. When he's
done, he takes the plate into the kitchen. Puts it in the sink. I
can't see what he's doing, but I hear him run water over it to
rinse off the crumbs. Then he's back, right in front of me,
arms crossed. He stares down at me, and I can't help but feel
like I'm about to be interrogated.

I start to sweat.

Where is Ian?

"Guns are cool." I'm babbling now. Guns are decidedly *not*
cool. They're dangerous, and anyone who owns them should
have to pass a yearly test to be able to keep them. I have a lot
of thoughts about guns, but I also have a very good feeling
that whatever I want to say isn't going to be appreciated by
my present company.

"Sure. I also learned interrogation tactics. Went into the
army as soon as I could. My old man was disappointed; he
thought I'd be a doctor like him."

"Family pressure is no joke." I relax a little. Maybe this
guy isn't a bad guy. He just wanted to get away from whatever
pressure he was under at home. I get it, I do. It's not that I had
parents who were involved or really cared about what I was
doing, but I read books. I've seen movies where teenagers act
out against their parents just so they can feel like they're
living their own lives.

"Yeah, good old Dad got what he wanted, though. My little brother became a doctor and a damn good one, too. Never afraid to push the boundaries of what could be done. He worked hard, played hard."

He's using the past tense while talking about his brother. The wall of ice that had been around my heart is thawing. Here's a big brother who joined the army to get away from family pressure from his dad, and then his little brother, who had done exactly what he's supposed to according to his dad, dies.

It's got to be rough.

"I'm really sorry to hear you lost him." I let my voice drop a little bit. One thing I've never been good with is platitudes when someone dies. I don't believe in heaven, but I do believe in hell for certain people. It's difficult for me to really connect with someone who's sad over losing a loved one.

I've lost people before, sure. But it wasn't ever a heartbreak for me.

Ryan opens his mouth to say something, but before he can, Ian pushes the door open, sending a cold blast of air around the room. He's struggling under a huge armload of wood, and I'm pleased when Ryan rushes over to take some of it from him.

"Thanks, man, I was getting a splinter through my glove." My husband's face appears above the pile. His cheeks are bright red from the cold, and he's grinning. "I know we got our wires crossed on when you were supposed to be here, but I have to admit it's really nice having someone around to help."

Ryan laughs. Claps him on the back. I notice his smile doesn't reach his eyes, but I don't think Ian sees this.

"What am I, chopped liver?" I force a smile to my face, pick up a log, and place it onto the fire. Immediately the flames burst back into life. "I can haul wood, you know."

"I know." Ian slings his arm around my shoulders. "You're great, Beth, you know that."

I snuggle into him. Ryan watches us, a dark expression crossing his face for a moment. I see it there, see the way his brow furrows, how his mouth turns into a slash, and then it's gone.

He smiles at the two of us. "Looks like you two are pretty much set for now, huh?"

Ian breaks away from me. He holds out his hand. Ryan shakes it, his hand dwarfing Ian's, making his fingers look tiny in comparison. "Thanks for taking care of the place, Ryan. I'm so lucky to have found you."

"That you are. Or maybe I'm the lucky one, to have found you."

He's speaking to Ian but looking right at me.

Any good feelings I had about the man are gone. I shiver, wrapping my arms around myself even though I'm right by the fireplace. What is it about this man that makes me so nervous? I'd swear on anything, even the Bible, that I haven't met him before.

"Do you want Beth to pack you some food for the trip home? I'll help you get the venison strapped to your snow-mobile. You won't need to worry about getting us that cooler back. I have no idea how long it's been out there in the shed." Ian laughs. It sounds easy, but I don't like the way Ryan is already shaking his head.

"You know what? On second thought, I think you might need a little bit more help around here. There's no reason for me to be dashing off so quickly. After all, like you said, Ian, we're so lucky to have found each other. Sometimes things just work out the way they're supposed to."

I can tell Ian's taken off guard by the way he tilts his head and blinks at Ryan. "Oh, but I'm sure you have things to do. Your family will want to see you, won't they?"

"Some things are worth waiting for." Ryan stretches, rolling his shoulders back and showing off his impressive muscles as he does. "Haven't you ever seen that? Besides, if it's worth doing, it's worth doing right."

It hits me who this man is.

I have to fight back a scream.

25

LIZZY

Three days go by after we have quesadillas for dinner before I get a chance to kill my husband.

I'm crunched for time now. Once he gets me back under the knife, I know I'll be too weak to try to hurt him for a while. He was so attentive to me when I had my nose job that I know how this will go. He'll flutter around me, fluffing my pillows, doing everything to make sure I'm happy and comfortable.

And then, as soon as I'm healed, we'll be right back where we started. I don't want to see the black lines appear on my body as he stands next to me in front of the mirror. I don't want him to mark off the parts of me that offend him, the parts he wants to change or cut off.

So I need to hurry.

There's nothing sharp in the house. There's nothing I can use to turn into a weapon. That's where I'm drawing a blank, and even though I know I need to do something to get out of here, I can't think of a single thing that will allow me to kill Zachary.

And then it all changes.

There are three boxes of new dishes and cutlery on the kitchen counter, the pictures on the side labels making it clear what's inside. I stare at them, then glance back at Zachary, trying to figure out the joke and what he wants me to do right now.

"Open them up." He sounds lazy. Looks it, even. As casually as possible, he's leaning against the kitchen counter, a glass of whiskey in his hand. I was surprised to hear him come home early from work, but it's not as if I was doing anything I wasn't supposed to do. Most of the afternoon I'd spent sitting on the sofa in the family room, staring at the wall.

I didn't eat. He stopped allowing me to eat lunch a while ago, telling me that he wanted to see if I could lose the stomach fat without surgery. Now my stomach is empty, hollow, painful, but I've learned to ignore the way it cries for food until dinner.

I turn my attention from him to the boxes. They're taped shut, and while a knife or some scissors would make opening them a lot easier, I'm not going to ask Zachary for something to use. He'll make a big deal out of unlocking where he keeps them and then hand them to me like a prison guard handing a dangerous inmate a potential weapon.

No, I'd much rather pick at the edge of the tape like an idiot than ask him for help.

It takes a few minutes, but I get the box open and flip the flaps to the side before reaching in and pulling out a stack of plates.

"New plates?" Of course they're new plates, I saw the picture on the side of the box. Still, part of me wouldn't have been surprised to open the box and find something totally unrelated to what I thought was inside. It would be just like him to put something terrible in the box for me to find.

"Unbreakable plates." There's pride in his voice, and I glance at him. "You can't break them. Try it."

I'm afraid to. Even though he's telling me to try to break the plate, I still hesitate, unsure of what he'll do if I actually succeed.

"Now, Lizzy. Break the plate. Or try, rather. You can't."

Anger washes over me, and I put the stack of plates on the counter. The one I pick up from the top of the stack is light, and I grip it by the edge before slamming it down on the edge of the counter.

It doesn't break.

I do it again, harder this time. I was wary before of any shards of glass or plastic or whatever the hell this is made of, but nothing splinters off. No shards come flying at me. Again I hit it, and again; then I try to snap it over my knee.

Nothing works.

He laughs, the sound a loud bark.

There's a roar in my ears, and I turn to look at him, breathing harder than I would like to admit. Maybe not having lunch every day is starting to wear me down. Maybe I need to try to sneak more food, but I don't know how to do that.

I shake my head to clear it. That's a problem for later, not right now.

"You can't break it, can you? God, I wish you could have seen yourself trying. You looked like an idiot." He laughs again, then puts his glass down on the counter to take the plate from me. "We're putting our plates and cutlery away. I don't want you to have access to anything you might be able to break and then use to hurt me. I know you've been thinking about it. I've seen the way you look at me."

Of course. There's always an ulterior motive with my husband, and it makes perfect sense he'd want to make sure I wasn't going to stab him with a shard. I swear, he's in my head. It's uncanny. I've always thought I was smart, but I'm starting to wonder if me getting away from my dad was a fluke. Was it just that he was so stupid, so drunk, so unassuming that I'd be able to do anything to protect myself that he had no idea what was coming for him?

Because that doesn't seem to be Zachary. It terrifies me, this thought that he might be able to stay one step ahead of me for the rest of my life.

And I don't want to consider how short that may be.

"Go ahead and put everything in the cupboards. We'll store the real stuff until we have company over and need it. I don't want you to get any crazy ideas." He pauses, walking over to me and taking a bit of my hair between his thumb and finger. He gives it a little tug, and I have to force myself to keep from breaking eye contact with him. "I know you were thinking about trying to hurt me the past few nights, Lizzy. But I'm better than you. Smarter."

I don't respond. He wants me to rise to his bait, but why? *Because he wants to push me to the edge and make me fight back.*

Following his instructions is the last thing I want to do, but I still do what he told me to, carefully swapping out the real plates and cutlery for this unbreakable stuff. There are even glasses that aren't supposed to shatter. I drop a wineglass on the floor. It bounces once and then rolls a few feet away from my toes before coming to a stop.

Zachary doesn't say a word. He watches me, his eyes locked on me, but although I know his mind has to be going a mile a minute, he doesn't make a sound. I feel like a lion in a zoo, on display, and my motions become jerky as I empty the cupboards, replace what was in them, box up the old dishes.

It hits me, as I'm putting a bowl in a box, that now would be a good time to try to attack. Slowly, so Zachary won't realize that I'm no longer working, I turn to look at him. I catch a glimpse of him out of the corner of my eye and freeze.

He's unlocked the knife cupboard and picked up a knife. I didn't even hear him open the locked cabinet where he keeps them, I've been so focused on doing what he wanted me to do. His grip on it is easy, relaxed, like he doesn't have a care in the world, but I have a very good feeling it would tighten faster than I could rush at him.

I keep working. It's uncomfortable having my back to him while knowing what he holds in his hand, but I really think I'm safe. Zachary doesn't want to kill me. He wants to make me into something other than I am. He wants to continue to torture me, control me. If he were to kill me, then he'd have to start over with someone else, and all the work he's put into training me would be wasted.

No, he's not going to kill me. He is going to keep me in line, though. That's what the knife is — a silent threat letting me know that it's all over for me the moment I do something that doesn't please him. I refuse to let him get the jump on me.

It takes half an hour, but I finally have all the dishes and silverware switched over to Zachary's new and improved unbreakable stuff. The boxes are all packed, the flaps closed, and I turn to look at my husband.

He still has the knife in his hand, and he glances at it before looking up at me. "I want you back in the basement, Lizzy."

It's a blow. I reach back, take hold of the counter's edge for support. "What? Why?" None of my plans that end in me killing him and escaping involve me living in the basement. If I'm going to make it out of here, it's going to be because he has a lapse and leaves a weapon — or something that could be used as a weapon — out in the house where I can reach it and use it.

"I don't trust you. You're squirrely, like you're planning something. You don't look happy. You can either go downstairs now, like I just said, or I can give you something to relax."

Something to relax. If he wants to drug me, then things are even worse than I thought. I can't let that happen. At the same time, there's a little voice in the back of my head telling me how nice it would be to finally relax, to have the edge taken off, to give up enough so that I'm not constantly trying to fight my way out of here.

I ignore that little voice.

"I'll go." I hold up my hands like that'll be enough to prove to him I'm not a threat. "I'm going, Zachary. You can put down the knife."

"I don't trust you, Lizzy. There's something about you that makes me nervous. You're different recently." He passes the knife to his other hand, and I inch my way out of the kitchen away from him. "I thought you would make this easier than you have been."

"I'm making it easy." Keeping my body turned towards him, I leave the kitchen. The basement door is just a few steps away, and I reach back for the doorknob. "I'm making it easy, Zachary. You don't have to worry about me, okay? Just let me go downstairs. Everything will be fine."

His footsteps are heavy as he walks towards me. "You just don't appreciate what I've done for you." He raises his voice and his hand.

Where the hell is the doorknob? My hand brushes against the wood door, but I can't find the handle that will allow me to escape him. Sweat breaks out on my brow.

Zachary approaches me faster now. There's a crease on his forehead that makes him look a bit feral. He's squinting, his mouth open, his empty hand reaching out for me.

And then it hits me that he's going to kill me. I thought I could string him along, make him comfortable enough that he would slip up and allow me the chance to kill him. I thought I was smart enough to make it out of here in one piece, but he's coming at me now, looking more like Jack Torrance than the handsome doctor who saved me from the side of the road.

Where is that fucking doorknob? I hit it with the back of my hand, hard, and wince, twisting my wrist around to close my hand on it. What is he doing with that knife? Is he going to kill me, or is this just one of his jokes, just him trying to scare me to get it through my head that I have none of the power here, none of the control?

"What are you doing, Zachary?" I hate the panic in my voice. I also hate the way it makes his eyes light up.

"I've been too easy on you!" He crows the words, a schoolyard bully who has finally cornered his prey well away from any teachers who might try to stop him from his nefarious plans. "That's the problem! I've been too easy on you, too loving, too kind. You don't seem to fully understand that I'm serious, that you'll do what I want you to, that you'll be the person I'm going to make you into, and that you'll do it without complaining!"

He's so close now, just a few feet away. My hand is firmly around the doorknob, and even though I want to throw the door open *right now* and flee, I force myself to take a deep breath, then another, and to wait, wait, wait until he's so close

—

And I throw the door open, kick my foot out, move to the side. My sudden movement takes him off guard, and he stumbles forward, the hand with the knife still out in front of his body, his head turning slowly to look at me as his foot catches against the side of mine.

DearGodIknowIdon'tpraybutletthiswork —

And then he's moving past me, the air current from his

body wrapping around mine, and the dark of the basement swallows him up while the sounds of his body slamming into the stairs reach my ears like music.

26

BETH

Nobody in town would have ever believed what my father did to me when I was a little girl, so I never bothered telling them. My mom died when I was seven. She was the lucky one, the one who checked out of this world before things could get even worse than they already were, and I hated her for it for a long time.

How could she do that to me? How could she knowingly leave me on this planet with the man who hurt me? But whenever I have those thoughts, whenever I think about railing and screaming about how unfair life really is, I remind myself that you don't choose to get cancer.

You're either lucky enough like her to get it and die quickly or unlucky enough like other people to suffer through it for the rest of their lives.

She was lucky. She died. I was unlucky, even though I didn't have cancer. Being left behind with my father was one of the worst things that could have happened to me.

He was violent. That's how every sob story starts, isn't it? My dad was violent, he hit me, he told me I was fat, or didn't let me date, or maybe he got drunk and the girl wakes up with his shadow in her doorway and she can't tell *was he coming or going?*

And of course, I don't mean to come across like I'm special, like I should get an award for living through what I did, but dammit, I survived.

And that's more than a lot of people can say.

Right now, staring at Ryan, I remember how I survived. It feels like all the air in the room has been sucked out, and while I know Ian and I need to deal with the fact that this guy clearly doesn't want to leave anytime soon and clearly has an ulterior motive for being here that my husband doesn't know — not just that, that he *can't* know — all I can think about is my dear old dad.

Freud would have a field day with what's going on inside my head, let me tell you.

The fire was easy to start. With all the alcohol in the house all the time and the fumes wafting from my dad's pores, nobody in town would have been surprised if the entire place just — *poof* — went up in flames. It was keeping him in the house while it burned down so he couldn't come after me that proved to be a bit more difficult.

For that, I had to rely on good old brute force, and even though I wasn't a particularly strong teenager, nor did I have a freakish surge of adrenaline that's apparently reserved for mothers who need to lift vehicles to save their children, the knife I had was really sharp, and he was drunk.

All things considered, if I did believe in God and in heaven, then I'd definitely have thanked him for the help that day. But I don't. I believe in my own drive to save myself and the fact that I was willing to burn up in our rickety old house if it meant my father wouldn't ever touch me again.

He'd gotten drunk. Again. But he wasn't that fall-asleep drunk that some men get when they've been in the bottle. I don't know why, but he was hanging on more than normal.

He was lucid, loud, angry. I had my bag packed and had stashed it in the woods behind the house. There wasn't much I wanted to take with me — my journal, an old necklace my mom had worn up until the day she died, some clothes.

Of course, I'd need clothes to be able to really make a run for it, and the little bit of cash I'd saved up working at the grocery store in town. My boss knew my dad was taking my money from me every payday, but I managed to keep some for my own.

Just enough to get out of town.

But I had to get rid of my dad. It wasn't enough for me to just walk away. Knowing that he was still out there and could come for me at any time wouldn't give me the peace I needed to survive the rest of my life. I needed him gone. I needed him dead. I needed to be able to rest easy knowing I wasn't going to turn the corner in a strange town one day and walk straight into him.

He had to die, or I wasn't ever going to be able to live.

Good parents are willing to put their lives on the line for their children. They want to do whatever it takes to keep their kids alive, but for me to live and for him to die, I knew I'd have to be the one taking matters into my own hands.

So I did. I didn't torture him — or I didn't *mean* to, some people could argue what I did to him was torture, but I dare them to say it to my face — I just stabbed him. Over and over, my tears and his blood mixing, then I doused the house with alcohol.

Lit a match.

And I never looked back.

I never liked the name my mom gave me anyway. *Elizabeth.* Like I was some little porcelain doll put there on a shelf when people were done playing with it. When *my father* was done playing. No, when I left town and ran, then it was time for me to put it all behind me, including my name.

So I moved. To Alabama. Changed my name. I kept it somewhat the same, not because I liked Elizabeth but because my mom picked it out for me. It wasn't her fault my name became something I was afraid to hear my father say. I became someone else, someone better, someone who wouldn't let people walk all over her.

And yes, I checked the paper from time to time, making sure nobody was going to be coming for me. I had to assume the cops knew he was murdered — they *knew* it, they had to — but it didn't seem to matter to them, not enough for them to start a national hunt for me. They looked; I hid.

And there's a part of me that honestly believes they didn't look as hard as they could have. That someone in town had to have known what was happening and was more than willing to turn a blind eye to the fact that I finally stood up for myself. It was either that or just sheer blind luck, but I don't believe in luck.

I believe in myself.

And after I moved, after I fled the scene and became someone I liked and could be proud of ... well, my past followed in a way I never expected.

And now it's somehow caught up with me.

"Beth, are you okay?" Ian tilts his head a little as he speaks, looking at me like you might look at a curiosity in the zoo. "You look a little bit pale, darling."

I swallow. Force a smile. "Sorry, I'm fine. I just got light-headed." I glance at Ryan. Look away again.

Only that's not his real name, is it?

"You know what? Maybe there's too much smoke in here. I just need to get some fresh air, and then I think I'll feel a bit better." I don't wait for Ian to respond before pushing past him to reach the door. I bump into him a little bit but make sure to stay well away from Ryan.

Outside, I bend over, grab my thighs. One deep breath,

then another. Closing my eyes, I think about the oxygen expanding my lungs, about my blood cells carrying it throughout my body, about it reaching my brain and helping me think clearer. More than anything I want to turn tail and run right now.

I have half a mind to make a break for the car. Get in. Drive away. Leave this all behind.

I'm halfway down the stairs before I realize I don't have boots on. My feet burn with cold, and I hurry back up to the porch, but I don't go in the house. I need time to think things through. I need to figure out what's going to happen next and how to handle Ryan.

It's obvious what he wants. It's obvious why he's here, why he hunted me down.

What isn't so obvious is what I'm going to do about it and how I'm going to protect myself.

"Think, Beth," I say, wrapping my arms tight around myself. "You gotta think, girl. You gotta pull yourself together and think this through."

We need to get this man out of the house, but I can't kick him out without Ian's help. And even if we tried ... I saw his muscles. There's no way the two of us could stand a chance against him if he wanted to stay. *And worse, he wants to stay.*

Since there's no good way to get him out of the house, then I'm going to need to get him alone. I need to find out what I can do to make him leave me alone, although I have a very good feeling he won't be satisfied with anything I try to offer him. If he's who I think he is — who I'm sure he is based on what he said and how he acts — he won't care one bit about money. He'll only care about revenge.

The door opens behind me, and I whip around. I need it to be Ian. I need my husband to be the one coming out to check on me, but it's Ryan, his bulk towering over me, his very presence sucking all of the air out of my lungs.

"Oh, Beth." He laughs, closes the door, then leans against it. Ian couldn't push through it to join me on the porch if he wanted to, not with Ryan blocking it the way he is. "You're a hard woman to track down, Beth."

I jut my chin out at him, trying to look braver than I feel. My hands are shaking, and I shove them deep in my coat pockets. Cold burns my feet, and I focus on how that feels rather than on how I want to throw up right now. Any thought I had of running is gone. I have to fight.

"But I found you." Even though I haven't answered him, he doesn't seem to care. "It took a while. Years, in fact. Imagine my surprise when I got out of the army and found out what you'd done. You're slippery."

"I did what I had to do." My heart hammers hard against my ribcage, and I pray he can't tell just how terrified of him I really am. It's one thing to plan to hurt someone to save yourself, but another entirely to imagine trying to save yourself from someone like Ryan.

"Did you now?"

I nod. My throat is tight. It burns when I swallow, like there are bits of glass embedded in my skin.

"Good to know, *Beth.* Let me tell you, I have a really wonderful idea of how the three of us are going to spend some time together."

27

LIZZY

I peer down the stairs into the dark. Without me looking, my fingers find the light switch, and I almost turn it on, but then I stop.

Wait. Listen.

"Zachary?" My voice sounds scared, and I latch onto that. What am I more scared of? That he's dead? Or that he's alive? The latter, definitely.

"Zachary?" I don't want to turn on the light, not because I'm afraid of seeing his broken body at the bottom of the stairs, but because I'm terrified of seeing him staring up at me, of him coming towards me, his hands outstretched. It's the stuff of nightmares.

My hand closes on the door. I could shut it, lock him down here, deal with it another day. If I waited long enough, then I'd know for sure if he was dead or not. He'd either come up to the door and call for me, or he wouldn't.

But where's his phone? I dash back into the kitchen, fear making me move as quickly as possible. I don't see it on the counter. Zachary is the type of guy to refuse to put his phone down if at all possible, which means he probably still has it in his pocket. Even if I lock the basement door, he'd be able to unlock it from his phone.

Or he could call for backup.

I have to get his phone from him.

I'm back at the door now, trembling with fear as I try to decide what to do. I have to go down there, have to get his phone. I don't think I have a choice, not if I want to make it out of here alive and without him coming for me.

"Or I could burn the place down." I revel in the thought for a moment, imagining flames leaping high in the sky as the place burns. I got away with it once, who's to say I couldn't again? For a moment I consider looking for a lighter.

But if I'm going to leave the house, I still need his phone to unlock the doors. If I set fire to the place now, it won't just be him whom the firefighters drag out, all crispy and black. It'll be me, too.

I can't let that happen.

"Zachary." One more time I call his name, hoping that he'll moan or move or something so I know what I'm getting into when I head down the stairs, but there's nothing, and I blink hard and bite my lower lip before turning on the light.

The basement is immediately illuminated. It feels like what I think a spaceship would be like, with light so bright you can see any little speck of dirt on the floor. I stare up at the light for a moment, letting it blind me from whatever else might be downstairs, then finally drop my gaze.

And I see my husband.

He's lying on his back, his arms splayed out from his body, one leg bent at a funny angle. I didn't hear the telltale crack of a bone as he crashed down the stairs, but would I have recognized it if I'd heard the snap? I don't know. I just know his leg is broken, in much the same way some people know they have cancer before they've been diagnosed.

So he's not going anywhere. Not easily, at least.

I drag my eyes up from his legs. See his arms again, but barely look at them. The knife is missing, and I feel a jolt of panic that he might have it hidden, that he might just be waiting for me to be stupid enough to come downstairs to brandish it at me, but then I finally register the one thing I was unable to see at first.

Bright red spreads out from his torso. The handle of the knife is clearly visible where it's lodged in his side. He must have fallen on it when he tripped, and now it's stuck there, making him ooze blood like a dying pig.

I descend a step. My hand is on the railing, the hair on the back of my neck sticking straight up. I'm ready to turn and run back up the stairs and out of the basement if I need to. I'll slam the door, block it off with furniture, try to keep him down here until he dies and I can steal his phone.

"Zachary." My voice is no louder than a whisper now, and I'm not sure he can even hear me. "Zachary, are you okay?"

A moan, soft enough to make me question at first if I even heard it, floats up to me, and I grip the railing tight enough that my fingernails sink into the wood. Zachary shifts, not really moving as much as sliding on the floor in an attempt to find a more comfortable position.

Can't be easy with a knife in your gut.

A laugh bubbles up in me, and I clap my hand down over my mouth.

His eyes flutter open. I watch as his mouth opens, then closes, a dying fish, but no sound comes out.

Now I'm practically running down the stairs. I step over his body, closing my eyes as I do, fully prepared for him to reach up and grab my ankle. He could yank me off my feet, pull the knife from his gut, put it in mine.

But I reach the other side safely, and I turn back, kneeling by Zachary. He's staring at me. This time, when he speaks, I'm close enough to hear him.

"It didn't hit anything major, Lizzy. I forgive you. Just get the phone out of my pocket. Call 911. I'll tell them what happened." Just a few short sentences, but they take a long time to come out. He takes slow, deep breaths between every word. The pain must be excruciating.

I touch the knife handle.

"Don't!" He gasps out the word. "Don't pull it out. I need help. I need a doctor. Call 911." His eyes flutter closed.

I look down at his leg, at how it's bent. I see the bulge of his phone in his pocket. Even though I don't want to touch him, I work it out of the fabric. He hisses in pain as I jostle his leg.

I jostle it again. Harder this time.

Another hiss.

The phone is in my hands now, and I grab his wrist, pressing his thumb to the side of the phone to unlock the screen.

"Call them." He never asks me to do things. He commands me.

I could. It would be so easy to call them, to unlock the doors. Hell, I could leave here right now when they came to get him. I could flee. He might come for me, but I bet he wouldn't. I bet he'd find someone else to hurt.

I can't let that happen.

"Lizzy. Dammit." Anger. Vitriol.

I know I can't let this happen to someone else. Instead of calling 911, I slip the phone into my back pocket and turn to the hospital bed. There are handcuffs hanging on the rails. Were they there before and I just hadn't noticed them? Or did Zachary come down here sometime just to add them for me? Are they the ones from the closet he showed me?

I don't know, but it really doesn't matter, does it?

"Come on." Bending, I grab under his armpits and start to

pull him back towards the bed. He's heavy, pure dead weight, and he screams as I jerk him backwards across the floor.

"What are you doing? You bitch! Call 911!"

"Not a chance." My teeth are gritted, and I don't know if he can understand me, but I really don't care. Pausing, I lean backwards, then give him a hard yank. He slides a few feet. Screams again.

"Keep it up," I tell him, unable to keep the mocking sound out of my voice. "Nobody can hear you, Dr. Pierce, and it's the weekend. Nobody will be looking for you until Monday."

Another yank. Another scream. His eyes flutter closed, and for a moment I think he's pretending until I realize that he's passed out.

Wuss, I think.

I'm panting by the time I get him to the bed; then I stop, considering if I have half a chance of lifting him up to the mattress. He's much bigger than I am, and while I would love to put him on the bed so I can more easily work, I make do with handcuffing his right wrist to the bedrail and leaving him on the floor.

Sick excitement rushes through me as I look down at my husband on the floor. I have no idea how long it will take him to bleed out, but hopefully the bleeding will slow and give me a chance to do what I really want. I'll bandage him up to keep him alive long enough to do what I want, then use his thumbprint again to use the phone to unlock the locked cabinets upstairs.

I'm not sure where he put all of the medical tools he showed me down here before, but I'll find them.

He wanted to change me, to make me perfect. But now I'm the one in control. I bend down, press his hand to the phone, then let it drop back onto the floor. It lands with a thud. He shifts, moaning slightly.

For a moment, I pause. *Who have I become?* Right now I'm

no better than him, no better than my father. I need to think about what I'm doing, need to mull it over, but I can't. Not now. Not when I have the opportunity to fix what Zachary did, to give him what he deserves.

Squatting next to him, I grab his chin and turn his face so he'll look at me when he opens his eyes. They flutter open just a moment, then fall shut again.

"Zachary." Letting go of his chin, I smack him lightly on the cheek. "Zachary, wake up."

Any fear I had of him is gone. I'm completely in control, just like I was when I took care of my father. Nothing can stop me now. I'll teach my husband a lesson, make sure he can't hurt anyone ever again, and then I'll leave.

Change my name. Change my life. Again.

"What are you doing?" He's in so much pain. I hear it in those four words.

"Zachary, I'm going upstairs to find the surgical tools you had down here." Standing, I look around the room, then finally see a marker on a table behind me. Grabbing it, I uncap it and squat back down. "Your cheekbones look good, but don't you think they could be more chiseled?"

The smell of the marker is sharp, bright. I take my time outlining his cheeks.

"That's a good start," I say. He whimpers, but I'm holding his chin again, squeezing it hard because I don't want to hear him make any noise. "We'll start with giving you a nicer contour, Zachary, okay? Then we'll see if there's any fat you want me to carve off." I grab his side, squeezing.

He hisses in pain, but I ignore him and walk to the stairs.

"We'll take our time working on this together," I say, tossing the words over my shoulder at him. "Remember, if it's worth doing, it's worth doing right." That said, I head upstairs.

I have tools to find.

28

BETH

He has a plan that will result in me dead, I know he does. But I have questions I need answered, and if there's one thing I've learned about dangerous men, it's that the longer you can keep them talking, the better the chance that you'll make it out alive.

Not that I have a lot of hope about that right now. Ryan towers over me in a way that doesn't just make me feel small, it makes me feel weak. Insignificant. I have no doubt in my mind — and I'm sure he's thinking the same thing — that he could easily crush me if he wanted to. I can't run. I can't fight him.

I have to outsmart him.

"You're not really Ryan."

He grins, showing me all his teeth. He's the Cheshire cat, here to play a little game, and I don't like the fact that the rules here don't seem to be the ones I've played by before. I'm at a clear disadvantage.

"Not really Ryan, no. Jacob."

My heart beats harder. I know that name. It was only mentioned in passing, but now my worst fears are confirmed.

Zachary's psycho older brother, the one who went into the army, the one who did it not because he wanted to save people, but because he wanted to be sanctioned to hurt them.

I married into a family of psychopaths and didn't know it at the time.

"Jacob." His name is metal in my mouth. Hard and unyielding, sharp like the blade of a knife. "Jacob, you tricked Ian into thinking you were some nice guy who would take care of his cabin for him. How did you set that one up?"

I need to keep him talking. Need to buy myself time to think.

And I really need Ian to stay in the house right now until I can figure this out.

"Oooh, close guess, but you're not quite right. I didn't meet your husband online. I've been watching your social media, though. You know, artsy people are the most obnoxious ones with posting every minute detail of their lives online. Your photographer husband sure shares it all, doesn't he?"

My stomach sinks. Yes, yes he does. And I hate it, but I've tried to overlook it because I love him so much.

"I found out about your cabin. About your trip up here. Ryan was so kind when I met him here at the cabin, so sweet with that stupid cat. He was easy to kill." Jacob cracks his knuckles. "I moved in. Waited. Pretended to be your caretaker, just a bumbling idiot who stayed a little longer than necessary to kill a deer for his family. It did feel good to do a little hunting, though. I love the wait, the chase. I love every part of the process." He pulls a face, then laughs.

I'm freezing. It's not just the biting wind or the snow I'm standing in, but a cold deep in my bones that makes me feel like I'm never going to be able to get warm again.

"You were in the cabin and then stayed out last night." My mind races while I try to figure out what this man is going to do. "Why? Why would you sleep in a cave, if that's what you were doing?"

"I was watching you. I wanted to get to know you. I skinned the deer, kept an eye on the two of you."

Chills race up my spine. "So, you ... what? Waited until you could meet us here to kill me, then watched me last night?" I'm trying to sound brave, but really I want to cry. After all I've done to try to have a good life, this is how it ends? It hardly seems fair that I took care of myself — twice saving myself from evil men — and I'm going to die like this.

"Oh, no, no." Another chuckle.

Each sound from his lips is sandpaper against my ears. I want to clap my hands over them and beg him not to speak another word. I can't stand the way he's looking at me, how he rubs his hands together, how he narrows his eyes like he's sizing me up.

Which, to be fair, is what he's been doing from the moment we met.

He's been sizing me up and definitely finding me lacking. I'm not a threat to him.

And I have to keep him thinking that.

"I don't want to kill you, *Lizzy.*" He sneers my name. "I want you to do something for me; then I'm going to make sure you're in jail for the rest of your life. You killed my brother, didn't you?"

There's no reason for me to respond. He's baiting me right now, and if he really knows as much as he says he does, then I just need to let his words roll off my back.

"But you didn't just kill him." He takes a step closer to me.

I glance at the door. Why isn't Ian coming out? Where is my husband? I'm torn between wanting him to come out here and potentially save me and wanting him to lock the door to save himself.

"I did what I had to do." What Jacob's saying demands all

of my attention. Lifting my chin, I stare at him. Lock my eyes on his. Dare him to push me.

"You didn't. You could have just killed him if it was really that bad. I've killed before, so I know how that goes. But you did more. You tortured him."

I freeze. No way. There's no way he knows that, no way he *can* know that. I was so careful only to cut his flesh. No nicks in the bone, no way that any autopsy would show the type of damage I caused his body, not when the fire was done. The fire was supposed to be cleansing, to eradicate all of my sins.

How does he know this?

"I watched it all." Another step closer.

I'm well aware that he could reach out and grab me by the neck. It wouldn't take much of an effort for him to simply snap my neck, toss me to the side. Then he could kill Ian.

Then it hits me what he just said. "What do you mean you watched it?" The chill I've been feeling is now overwhelming. I'm shaking, but not just from the cold. I'm terrified. Yes, I've been scared before. Multiple times in my life, in fact.

But never like this.

"I watched it. I watched you torture my brother, but it was too late. He'd set up the cameras and given me an access code to see what was happening. I was ... working at the time. I didn't see it until it was too late."

No.

"Do you want to know the ironic thing?" He doesn't give me a chance to respond, although I don't think I could speak even if he held a gun to my head and tried to force me. Leaning forward, he whispers in my ear, "I was off doing the same thing you were. We're the same, you and I."

Cold creeps up my spine. Of course I know that some people in the army are truly evil, just like I know there are people who hide their crazy behind business suits and a polished façade to prevent others from finding out the truth about who they really are.

Or they hide behind scrubs.

But to know that I'm face-to-face with someone from the army, someone trained in techniques like the ones I've only dabbled with, is terrifying. I did it because I had to.

He does it because he loves it.

"So now you and I are going inside. I have a surprise set up for you in there. You want to play with the big dogs? I'll walk you through how to really hurt someone. Ian's all ready for you. You'll see what I mean."

God, no. I'm terrified to walk in that door, to see what he has set up for me, because I think there's a part of me that already knows. But what choice do I have?

Jacob swings his arm out to the side, gesturing to the door. "Let's move it, sunshine. I want to get this started. I'll teach you a few things. Then I'm going to call the police, send you to jail where you belong."

My mouth is dry. I lick my lips to try to speak, but there's no moisture there. Bracing myself, I walk past him in the front door, half-hoping, half-afraid Ian will be standing there. He'll be laughing, because he's always happy, and he'll want to know what's wrong.

At the same time, I can't face my husband. I can't tell him what I did, and I certainly can't hurt the man I love. Taking a deep breath, I step inside the cabin, an apology already forming on my lips. I don't know what I'll say to Ian to try to make him understand how sorry I am for everything that's happening, but I'll come up with something.

I have to.

But he's not standing here. Confused, I look around the room. "Where ..." But that's all I get out before my eyes fall on my husband.

He's sitting on a straight-back chair in the middle of the

living room, his body strapped to it like luggage on top of a car. There's a hood over his head and huge headphones on his ears.

"What did you do to him?" I'm desperate, and I turn, clawing at Jacob's chest. He's towering over me and shuts the door firmly behind him. Locks it. Laughs.

"I injected him, got him woozy, got him ready for you. Amazing on-the-job training I received to learn how to do these sorts of things. He can't hear you, not with the music playing."

Music. I walk to Ian, my heart thudding harder with every step. When I reach him, I hesitate, then lean down next to him to try to hear —

"Touch him and I'll kill you right now." Jacob's voice is light. He sounds like the two of us are bantering about where to eat lunch. *Oh, Beth, if you suggest we go out for pineapple pizza one more time, I'll rip your arms right off your body and beat you with them.*

I freeze. Take a slow, deep breath. Just a few inches from Ian and I can hear the sound of loud rock music through the headphones. "Is he okay?"

Jacob shrugs. "He's drugged. He's going to wake up. Sooner rather than later."

What does he mean by that?

29

LIZZY

I don't want to push my luck staying in the house with Zachary any longer than is safe. It's one thing to spend all day Saturday and Sunday morning showing him exactly what I think of his plan to perfect me, as he always said, but another to stay into Monday when people are finally going to notice that he's gone.

I heft his phone as I stand in the kitchen, trying to decide what to do. This house is great. Now that Zachary's no longer alive, I could live here and be very happy. I know I could make new memories and get rid of the old ones that I made here with my husband, but sticking around isn't the best option for me.

You don't just not show up for your job at the hospital and not expect people to come looking for you. As much as I'd like to think I could hide out here without someone finding out what I did, the longer I wait, the greater the chance I end up in prison. That just can't happen.

It is a shame to burn down such a gorgeous house, however. Zachary's phone beeps, and I look down at the screen, pleased to see a text from Carla. She'd been so surprised when I texted her earlier. It was easy to pretend to be Zachary and tell her, tearfully, that I'd left.

She thinks Lizzy bailed on him in the middle of the night. He's been depressed but doesn't want to see anyone. What she doesn't know is Lizzy is dead to me, and I'm already reinventing who I'm going to be in the future.

Are you sure you don't want Eric to come by and carpool to work?

"Not a chance," I whisper, my fingers flying over the screen. I have to keep them away from the house a little bit longer, but I need them to really worry about Zachary. "I'm taking the morning to myself," I say as I respond. "Tell him thanks, but I'll be in later and will meet him for lunch."

There. Plans are made. People will be looking for Zachary, but he's such a private person that it only took a little convincing this weekend to keep Carla and Eric from coming over. They are worried, like any good friends would be, but not so worried that they want to change their morning plans.

Maybe if Zachary hadn't been such a psycho. Maybe if he'd cultivated friendships, someone would have come looking for him by now. But he didn't, and they didn't, and now I get to finish my plan and get the hell out of here.

There's a cigar on the counter, and I cut it, light it, and take a few puffs. Who knew Zachary was such an aficionado? He never shared this part of his life with me, but I've certainly enjoyed unlocking all the locked cabinets and cupboards in the house while he was in the basement. It gave me a chance to really get to know the man I married, and I can say with certainty that he needs to die.

The smoke is thick, rich, and I cough a little as I head downstairs with the cigar. Everyone knows how much he likes scotch. And whiskey. And tequila. I have to make it look like he was drunk, like he accidentally started a fire, and it got out of control.

It's the only way I'll be free of him and be able to live my own life.

I crack open bottle after bottle of his liquor, pouring them around the house, making sure to concentrate a lot of it on his body. I was careful with my cuts while I made him perfect.

Hopefully nobody will know that he was dead before he burned up. Sure, the police will look for me, but I'm a ghost. I'll be long gone by then, and I don't ever intend on coming back to Alabama.

Before dropping the cigar by my husband and starting the fire with the lighter in my pocket, I checked that the sprinkler system was offline. It's a silly little thing to be able to do, but I guess if you're making repairs or had an accident in the kitchen, you don't want water to fling from the sky.

Nothing can save this house, just like nothing could save Zachary.

Bending down, I tuck the cigar between Zachary's fingers. He still has all of those. The phone is next, just to make sure it burns to a crisp, as well. Everything I need to unlock to get out of the house is open. I'm free to go for the first time since walking in here.

Then I stand. Step back. Light the lighter.

Throw it.

I have to hurry out of the basement. Maybe I'm being stupid and cutting it too close. Maybe I should have thought this through a bit more than I did, but at this point there's no turning back and no way that I would even if I had a second chance. I race through the house, grabbing the keys to my car before running into the garage.

I've never actually driven it. It's brand new, with only a few miles on it from bringing it home from the dealership, but Zachary thought it was worth the price for him to be able to make it look like we were a normal couple. The engine purrs to life, the leather seat is smooth to my touch, and I back out, pausing the car to close the garage door once I'm clear of it.

A huge part of me wants to stick around and watch the house burn down. We're far enough from any neighbors that I don't think the smoke will be visible until it's too late. Then it will take firefighters a little while to get here, longer to put out the flames, even longer to find Zachary in the basement.

I wonder if the house will collapse in on him.

I wonder how long it will be before they start to look for me.

It doesn't matter. I ran once. I'll run again.

But this time, I want to be done running. I want to find a nice man, get married to him, settle down. I don't need a man — no woman really does, if we would just start being honest with ourselves about what we're capable of — but I want to be married. I want someone to take care of me just because I've never had that.

I don't have a phone, so I just start driving north. I need to get as far away from this place as possible before the police are called. I'll dump the car in a bit and buy a junker. There's a huge wad of cash in the bag I stuffed under the passenger seat. As soon as I get out of Alabama, I'll switch cars.

Maybe cut my hair. I could dye it in the sink of a gas station bathroom. Isn't that what women typically do in the movies when they're on the run? It always seemed so silly to me, like a trope that writers put in there because it's not something that ever actually happens, but why not?

And then north, but not too far. I don't like the cold. I want to be somewhere that's warm at least some of the time.

I hit the interstate, taking care that I'm not going any

faster than the other cars on the road. I'll blend in, make sure no cop looks twice at me.

And then, to where? South Carolina is too warm for me. They don't get any snow, and I want at least a little for the first time in my life. Maybe North Carolina. There was that crazy man, the Olympic bomber, who lived in the mountains there for a long time. I won't eat from a dumpster like he did, but if it was good enough for him to hide out there, it should work for me.

To North Carolina, then. To a new life. To a future where I don't have to kill the man I thought loved me.

To a future where I don't want to hurt him.

I press down harder on the gas.

30

BETH

Jacob presses the knife into my hand. It's perfectly balanced, with a short blade and a light handle that feels great when I heft it. I grip the handle and then turn on the man behind me, adjusting my grip just a little bit, sizing him up ...

Maybe if I act quickly, I can take him off guard. Maybe I can stop this nonsense before it really ramps up, before I have to do anything to the sweet man tied to the chair in front of me.

I can't let this continue.

Jacob raps his knuckles against his chest. "Ballistic vest. You try to stab me and you'd better hope you can ram that piece of metal all the way through it before I grab you and snap your neck. Plenty of men have tried. None have succeeded."

What he says makes me reconsider. It was one thing to kill my dad. To kill Zachary, who would have bled out anyway had I just walked away. They were both at a disadvantage, and as much as I'd like to think it isn't true, Jacob here has the upper hand. He's bigger. Stronger. Faster.

More insane.

"I can't hurt him." I swallow, fighting back tears. "You can't make me hurt him. I love him!" My voice rises to a wail, but he doesn't seem fazed.

"You hurt Zachary."

"He was a monster." My grip on the knife is getting sweaty, and I switch the blade to my left hand. Wipe my hand on my pants. Switch it back. "You have to see that. He was insane. He locked me up, never let me leave the house, limited what and when I could eat. He forced me to have a nose job even though I didn't want one. He was going to carve me up to make me perfect. But I was fine!"

"Every woman would have loved to be in your position." Jacob is maddeningly calm. He exudes confidence, that of a powerful man who knows he's going to get exactly what he wants, and there isn't anything a single person can do to stop him. "All you had to do was be better, and he would have loved it. He worshipped you."

"Please." I hate begging. Hate feeling like I'm not in control. "I didn't have a choice. I didn't have a choice!" I'm screaming the words at him now.

He steps back, and for a moment, I think I've won. His hand dips into the pocket of his pants, and I stiffen, sure he's going to pull another weapon on me, sure he's going to make me fight him.

I can do it. My muscles tense as I prepare myself. There's a buzzing in my head, and I know I'm going to die, but I won't hurt Ian. I won't do it. I love him.

Jacob pulls a small disposable camera from his pocket.

I blink. The last time I saw one of those had to have been in high school. The prom committee set them out on all the tables in the gym so people could snap pictures of each other while dancing and eating. Honestly, I had no idea they even made the things anymore.

"Smile for me." He raises the camera to his eye and presses the button. The shutter sound is so loud I flinch. "I've been working on taking better pictures. We can critique your work together before you go to jail. How does that sound?"

"Please, no." I'm whimpering. Even though I know he's going to be angry, I loosen my grip on the knife and let it fall to the floor. It clatters to the ground.

"Pick it up."

"No." I mouth something else, but no sound comes out. Behind me, I hear Ian stirring. He shifts his weight on the chair, the legs scraping against the floor. I turn to watch, horror rising in my gut as I see my husband struggle against his binding.

"Touch him and I will kill you. Pick up the knife, Lizzy. Let me see what you're made of."

His words freeze me in place. I hadn't even noticed I was halfway to my husband, my hand outstretched like I could free him. When I turn back, I'm not surprised to see Jacob holding the camera in one hand, another knife in the other.

This one is larger. The blade is heavy, curved.

I pick up the small knife. Tears drip off my chin, but I don't bother to wipe them away. "Please, no. I'll do anything. Please just let me go. Let Ian go. Anything, okay? I'm sorry about Zachary. I'm sorry! I shouldn't have done it, you're right. It was a mistake. It was just me being desperate, and I messed up. I'll leave — we'll leave — and you'll never see us again. Just let us go. Let me take him."

Jacob ignores me. He strolls past me to Ian. When he touches my husband on the thigh, Ian jumps. He cries out, the terror in his voice so obvious that it makes me want to throw up.

"Right here," he tells me, patting my husband on the thigh. "Right here is where you stab him first. Both legs. You'll miss any important blood vessels. Now, Lizzy. I'm getting bored."

"No." Tears stream down my face as I look up at Jacob. "No, I won't do it. I love him, don't you see that? He doesn't deserve this! I do!" My mind races as I try to come up with a plan that will save the both of us, but I can't think straight.

Jacob moves faster than I would have thought possible. He steps behind me, looping his arm around my neck. "You'll do it like you did to my brother. Do it now, Lizzy."

"I didn't want to!" The words escape in a sob. "He made me do it. If I didn't stop him, he was going to kill me." It's hard to breathe, but I suck in tiny snatches of air. He's not pressing hard enough on my neck to kill me, just to make the edges of my vision blur.

"You didn't have to torture him." There's a note of anguish in his voice, and I fixate on it, knowing what he said is right. "You didn't have to go as far as you did."

I didn't. But I did.

"I know!" I'm not going to be able to keep him talking long enough to save myself, but maybe, if I hurt myself, if I kill myself, I'll be able to save Ian.

I twist in his grip. His arm tightens around my neck, and now I really can't breathe, but my arm is free, and the knife is not pointed towards Ian, and I swing the knife down, slicing across my skin.

Hot pain shoots from the cut, racing up my arm, and I gasp, the knife finally falling free from my hand. I hear it clatter against the floor, and at the same time, the pressure on my neck releases.

"What the hell are you doing?" Jacob screams at me. Grabbing me by the shoulders, he whips me around to face him. His spit lands on my skin, but I don't flinch away.

"I love him," I say, in between gasps of air. My lungs burn like I'm never going to get enough oxygen ever again. I feel tears racing down my cheeks, but I don't move to brush them away. My arm aches, the cut painful. Blood runs down my arm, and I close my eyes, take a deep breath.

I have to try to keep my wits about me.

"Pick it up." Jacob's voice is all gravel and broken glass, and I have to force myself to look at him. "Now, Lizzy. Pick. It. Up."

"I won't hurt him. Please, I made a mistake! Your brother, he hurt me, he —"

Jacob doesn't wait to hear what I'm going to say. He moves quickly, grabbing the knife and pressing it into my good hand. Without thinking, my fingers close on the handle.

I look down at it, almost surprised to see it there.

"Don't think for one second that killing yourself is going to get you out of this," he tells me. "It won't save him. I can stay here as long as necessary until you finish this. Now do it."

I can't focus on anything. My head pounds, and my thoughts feel fuzzy.

I feel like I'm in a dream as I put the tip of my knife against Ian's leg. "I'm so sorry," I say, the words coming out of me in a rush. "Ian, I'm so sorry." He can't hear me over the sound of the music pumping into his ears, and thank God for that. I don't think I could stand it if I had to look him in the eyes later and know that he knew the truth.

I'm a monster, but I never meant to hurt him. I love him.

"Do it, Lizzy. Do it, or I'm going to start by breaking every single one of your fingers."

I close my eyes.

I don't see a way out.

My husband screams as I do what Jacob told me to. The sound is horrible, and I'm sobbing now, my knife rising, then lowering, my hand taking over as my brain shuts off. I want this to stop, but I don't know how to get out of here if I don't do what Jacob told me to. Ian keeps screaming as I stab one thigh, then the other, my hand now slick with his blood.

He gasps one last time, then is silent, his head lolling forward as it droops down to his chin.

Oh, God, Ian. I'm so sorry.

I think for a moment I've killed him, and I stop, horrified, the knife still clutched in my hand, my fingers locked around it like claws. I step away from him. Enough. I did what Jacob asked, but I can't do more. I *won't* do more.

But still I clutch the knife. Could I even drop it if I wanted to? I feel like it's become part of me, an appendage that has always been there but has been hidden up until this very moment.

"You're doing great. He just passed out." There's a click and a whir, and I turn. Jacob lowers the camera. "More. Keep going, Lizzy. I want to see you do what you did to my brother."

I don't think I can. Turning, I throw up, the vomit splattering on the floor. I'm heaving now, the knife clattering to the floor as I grip my thighs and empty everything out of my body. It hurts, my muscles cramping as I heave, lights flashing in my eyes. They're bright, growing brighter, and for a moment I think I'm going to pass out.

Jacob's hand clamps down on my shoulder. "Don't move. Don't make a fucking sound."

I freeze, still bent over. My eyes are open, but the lights are still visible. They're growing brighter, flashing around the room of the cabin, blue and red mingled together in some parody of help arriving. It's sick, what my mind is doing to me, and I hate myself for almost thinking someone is here to help.

"I'll deal with them. You stay right here, do you understand? Move one inch — *one inch* — and I will gut you. I swear I'll get to you before they stop me." He stares at me.

I look back at him, struggling to make sense of what's happening. I know I have a knife. I've been hurting my husband. *Oh God, Ian.* Turning, I look at him. I can't see his face but I can see him breathing. Each rise and fall of his chest is so slow I'm not sure if he's going to make it. I hate the way each little breath sounds more like a wheeze than anything else. Even though I know I need to concentrate on what Jacob is doing, I can't tear my eyes away from Ian.

I hear footsteps behind me. The door opens. Jacob's voice, low and reassuring. I'm stuck in glass, completely frozen, unable to move. All I can do is listen as his words wash over me.

If I could move my feet, then I could rush to the door. Maybe I could interrupt, tell the person outside what's really going on. It has to be a police officer; that's the only thing that makes sense. The lights in the windows, the banging on the door.

"Oh, yeah, I'm sorry, you can tell my wife I just got held up." Jacob laughs.

My mind races as I try to imagine him with a wife. I didn't see a ring on his finger, but maybe he just doesn't wear one. Still, why would the police be here to check on him? Why would his wife call and ask them to come out here?

Through the window I see a vehicle parked in front of the cabin. It's a huge truck with giant tires and a light bar on the top going crazy.

"So you are Ryan McKinney?" A man's voice.

"Yes, sir. You tell that sweet wife of mine to stop worrying." Jacob again. Lying to the cop.

It hits me what happened. Ryan has a wife, and she's missing him. Of course she'd call the cops to come out here and try to find him. He's dead, his body dumped somewhere in the snow, probably not to be found until the spring melt.

My stomach rolls again, and I clamp my lips shut, trying to keep from throwing up again.

"You got it. I'll call her as soon as I get back in service. You sure you're okay out here? Got food? Water?"

"I have everything I need." There's a current of evil in Jacob's words, but I don't expect the officer to pick up on it. I'm the only one who really knows how dangerous this man is. I'm staring at him, taking in his broad shoulders, the hard lines of the ballistics vest he told me he was wearing.

I can't stab him in the back.

But I have to stop him.

If I cry out now and the officer comes in, Jacob will kill him, then Ian. Then me. I won't stand a chance at saving Ian, and there's no way he'd let me walk out of here. I have to time it perfectly.

If it's worth doing, it's worth doing right. The thought almost makes me laugh.

I take a step toward Jacob, hedging my bets that I won't step anywhere that will make noise. We haven't been in the cabin long enough for me to determine where all the loose boards are, where I can put my weight without making any sound and where I can't, but I have to risk it.

Another step. Then another. The knife is in my hand, the blade pointed away from me. It's slick with blood, but growing sticky. It's part of me.

Another step.

Jacob and the officer are still talking. I need the cop to stay for another moment, to wait a bit longer, to linger just in case I don't have the time to get close enough. But now he's closing the door, the officer is stamping his boots as he turns away from the door and hurries down the stairs, and I do the only thing I know to even though I'm not sure I'm going to succeed.

I lunge, throwing all of my weight at Jacob. He's bending,

looking out the crack in the door, a small strip of his neck exposed.

I hear the truck start up. It growls to life, the roar so loud that there's no way the officer can hear anything else. The rumble of the engine drowns out all other sound, and even though I can't read the officer's thoughts, I know what they are.

Getoutofherecallhiswifegethomeandhaveadrink.

The knife finds its target, and I shove it deep, praying it will be enough to at least stun this monster, to stop him. The blade catches on bone, and I swear, fumbling with the handle. I yank it back, and blood pours out over my hand.

31

North Carolina Mountain Times

Set for release December 29

After a harrowing trip to upstate New York, where Ian and Beth Myers were set to clean out his family's cabin, the couple has returned, alive and well, though with scars that won't soon heal.

The unlucky couple was in their cabin when they were attacked by a madman who had previously broken into their cabin and murdered the caretaker. This man held the two of them hostage. After tying Ian to a chair and repeatedly stabbing him, he was only stopped when Beth managed to escape being locked in the bedroom and attack him.

Luckily, the couple was able to flee the cabin and call police. Officers arrived on scene, set to arrest Jacob Pierce, but found him already deceased. Ian was taken to the local hospital, where he was kept for three days until it was determined he would make a full recovery.

Both Ian and Beth consider the fact that they're home and well as a Christmas miracle. While they had originally planned to sell the cabin to pay for IVF treatments, they now just want to be rid of the property and have donated it to the National Park Service. As the land butts up to a national park, it will easily be added to the Adirondack State Forest and open to the public early next year.

It will be a few weeks before Ian, who teaches photography at West Brevard High, and Beth, who works at Flowers by Maisy, are back to work. In the meantime, they're spending as much time together as possible healing, are grateful to be alive, and are planning the next chapter of the lives. After a life-threatening experience, they're both just happy to have the ability to celebrate each new day.

To donate to the GoFundMe set up for Ian's medical bills, click the link below.

To donate to the GoFundMe set up for IVF so the couple can start a family, click the link below.

32

BETH

The cup of coffee on the counter has gone cold, but it still smells amazing, and I carry it to the microwave to nuke it. Ian would laugh at me if he saw me do this, but old habits die hard, even though heating it up like this instead of getting new coffee will only result in it tasting stale.

As it heats, I turn, lean against the counter, and take in the kitchen. It hasn't changed that much since when Ian and I were first married. There are new prints on the wall, huge photographs Ian took that we had professionally blown up. For a long time after we first got married, he kept asking me to try my hand at photography with him. That stopped out of the blue, thank goodness.

Ever since we were in the NY cabin together, I want nothing to do with photography.

I'm glad he enjoys it so much and can make money from it, but I don't want to be behind a camera. I don't want to spend long hours in his darkroom with him. I can barely even remember the only time I ventured down there. It must have been when we were first dating and he wanted to show me his work. He certainly hasn't invited me down there recently.

I remember the irrational fear that he was going to lock me in when he took me to his darkroom. It had taken me two glasses of wine to make it down the stairs with him, but now I know his darkroom is just that. There aren't any surgical tools, no hospital bed waiting for me. There's no ghost of the man I murdered haunting the basement.

That's all in the past, and every day it gets farther behind.

The microwave beeps, and I gratefully take my cup out. When I take a sip, I wrinkle my nose. I wouldn't admit it to Ian, but he was right. This tastes terrible. Moving quickly, I dump it down the sink and start a fresh pot.

It's been two years since everything at the cabin happened, and while I thought for sure I'd go to jail, or Ian would leave me at the very least, I didn't. And he didn't. The hood, the headphones, everything convinced him that Jacob had been the one attacking him. It was easy to explain away the blood on me and the cut on my arm by telling him I'd been trying to protect him, trying to keep him from bleeding out.

Everyone believes me. Ian believes me because he wants to. I know he couldn't handle the thought that I would actually turn on him, that I would want to hurt him. He can't fathom the thought that I'm not the perfect wife.

Because I am. I have been since the day we said our vows, and now I'm the perfect mother. Thanks to that GoFundMe one of the teachers at his school set up for the two of us, we have Molly.

The sound of her stroller squeaking makes me turn from where I'm watching coffee drip into the pot. "Hey, you two off somewhere? I was just making coffee."

Ian smiles at me. It's tight, though, which tells me he's stressed about something. I'm not sure what it is. It could be anything from a photography student at the school not understanding an assignment to his work not turning out the way he wants it to.

"Actually, yeah. I'm taking Miss Molly here out on a stroll. I've been in my head with my photography. It's more work than I thought to take digital pictures of everything and upload them to the cloud. That way, though, if something ever happens, I'll still have copies."

Ahh, I see it now. Good. Hopefully a little walk in the cool air will help him focus. Creative people face burnout. If he needs to go on daily walks to head it off, then I hope he will. Even though I've never faced burnout like that, I do know how being creative day in and day out can wear on you. He needs a break.

Normally I'd ask to go along with him, but I'll stay home and see if I can work on a surprise for him instead.

"Your head is just so amazing," I tell him, walking over to say goodbye to Molly. "I get wanting to be in there all the time."

Another smile. It's less tight this time. He wraps his arms around me, pulling me to him. "Tell me how much you love me."

I laugh. It's a strange request, but one he started after we survived the cabin together. In his mind, I'm a hero. I want to keep it that way.

"I love you more than anything in this world, Ian. Except Molly." We both laugh. "I'd do anything to keep you safe. Anything."

He kisses me again. Heat flushes through me, but I pull away after a moment. As much as I love being with my husband, I don't want to be the reason he doesn't get to take the walk he wants to go on.

I bend over Molly's stroller and tweak her toes, then her fingers, then finally lean down close to her and kiss her perfect little nose. She gurgles up at me, her approximation of a laugh, and I laugh back, then tuck her in. Sure, her blanket will get kicked off her and out of the stroller before she and Ian make it a block away, but it doesn't matter.

Being a mom is the most important thing to me. I love Molly, and I love Ian, and I'll do anything to protect the two of them. Ian has to know that even if he doesn't know exactly how far I'm willing to go to keep him safe.

"You two have a good walk," I say, grabbing Ian by his open jacket and pulling him to me. "I love that you want to take her on a little stroll, just the two of you." Bouncing up on the balls of my feet, I give him a kiss. "If I can do anything for you, I want you to let me know. You're my person, Ian."

He kisses me back. Glances down at Molly. "I love you, Beth, more than anything. And thanks for letting the two of us go off on our own." With that he pats his pockets. "Phone, keys, wallet. We'll be back; don't worry about us."

"I don't," I say as I watch them leave. The front door slams as they go outside. It's incredible, but with Ian, I don't worry about a thing. He's everything to me. I knew from the first time I met him just how incredible he is, and having to hurt him when we were in New York almost did me in. I'll do anything to protect my family, and I proved that to myself by killing Jacob.

I lied to the police. I lied to Ian. He can never know about it because he wouldn't understand. As much as I hope he would, there are some things that you just can't understand if you're not the person living them. As much as we love each other, he wouldn't be able to wrap his mind around me hurting him to save him. I just know it.

It takes a special kind of person to survive what I have and to be willing to hurt someone you love to save them. The knowledge that I'm the one who hurt him so badly tears me apart.

But I didn't do it because I wanted to. I did it because I had to. There's a huge difference, and there aren't many people in this world who would be able to understand it. I love my husband, but there's no way he'd understand that I did what I had to in order to keep him safe.

The coffee finishes brewing, and I pour myself a cup, then stir in some sugar and add creamer from the refrigerator. There. That's better. That's what I needed to get out of my head. Just like Ian, I get lost in my thoughts sometimes. And just like him, it's usually photography that has me unable to focus on anything else.

But I'm not worried about my art. I'm worried about the camera Jacob was using to take pictures of me hurting Ian. He snapped some; I know he did. But after the dust settled and Ian was out of the hospital, we went back to the cabin to clean it up. I hadn't left his side at the hospital — I couldn't, out of a combination of fear of something he might say and the worry that he would die while I was gone.

I never found the camera. I swear, I looked everywhere for it while Ian packed up the few things we needed to take from the cabin to come back home. I wanted to bring Mya home, but Ryan's widow was thrilled to have her back. She'd gone to visit her sister, so he'd taken Mya to the cabin with him. Ryan never made it home, but his widow was thrilled to see Mya again.

But it's not her I'm worried about. It's that blasted camera.

It's impossible the police found it because they would have developed the photos by now, I really feel like they would. Ian never mentioned the camera. I didn't see him picking it up, so I keep telling myself he doesn't know about it. Its very existence and what's on that film is the sword of Damocles hanging by a thread right over my head, the very knowledge of its existence enough to make me sick.

Should I have come clean? Maybe. *Probably.* But how was

I to look my husband in the face and tell him I stabbed him? Each day that passes makes it that much harder for me to even think about telling him the truth.

I guess I still could. At least once a week I wake up in the middle of the night in a cold sweat. I think about the camera Jacob had. I wonder where it is.

Ignoring it and hoping for the best is the wrong thing to do, but people avoid their problems all the time, don't they? Women know they feel a lump, but they don't go to their doctor. Men have a feeling their wife might be stepping out on them, but rather than rock the boat, they pretend like everything is fine at home.

It's what I've been doing. For the most part, I think I'm doing okay.

It's just when I wake up, afraid Jacob is *right there* in the room with me, afraid Ian will know the truth, that I feel like I'm coming apart at the seams.

I'll keep lying to myself. Lying to my husband. It's worked so far, and I have to hope it will continue to do so.

No matter what, I keep telling myself I had nothing to do with what happened to Ian. If I say it enough, maybe I'll believe it.

Shaking my head, I take another sip of my coffee.

Worrying about the camera won't do any good. It's gone. I don't know where it is, and while knowing would give me peace of mind, I'm not going to focus on it for too long. All that will do is make me want to pull out my hair.

It's obvious I need to slow my thoughts down, and I take a deep breath. Hold it. *One, two, three, four, five.* Exhale. *One, two, three, four, five.*

Again.

Counseling isn't an option for me because I know where I'd end up as soon as I started spilling my guts about all the things that have happened to me in my life. I've downloaded a few apps on my phone to help me learn to control the beginnings of panic attacks and to help me keep a closer eye on my moods. My life is going perfectly right now, and there's no way I'm going to let anything stand in the way of me enjoying it, including myself.

Another sip of coffee. More breathing.

Soon a calm washes over me that's probably a combination of the caffeine hitting my system as well as a little extra oxygen to my brain. Still holding my mug, I head towards the basement door. It's right off the kitchen, tucked in an easy place for me to ignore it exists, and while I normally wouldn't go down into the darkroom, I have a project I'm working on for Ian.

Our anniversary is coming up, and I want to have some of his photographs framed for him. Most of the ones we have hanging in the house are older shots he's taken from when we were first married and when Molly was born. He has to have newer shots downstairs that I can take and frame for him. The one time I went into the darkroom with him, I was impressed and a little surprised about how organized everything is.

He had his fresh shots hanging like laundry on a line across the back wall of the room. Under them was a trough where the chemicals can drip as they dry, but I'm not interested in what new shots he's taken. I know he has boxes of older photographs, and that's what I want to get into.

I want something recent, but not so recent he'd notice it missing from the drying line.

Should be easy to find.

Right outside the basement door, I stop and put my mug down on the floor, making a mental note where it is so I don't kick it over when I come back upstairs. This shouldn't take long, and I'm hoping my coffee will still be warm by the time I get back.

At the bottom of the stairs is a thick curtain that I have to push to the side to enter the actual darkroom. Before doing that, I flick the light switch next to me to turn off the light on the stairs. Immediately I'm plunged into a deep dark, but I'm not scared.

I know what's down here. Ian isn't plotting anything terrible. He's not going to hurt me.

Pushing the curtain aside, I let it fall shut behind me, then find the next light switch. This one turns on a red light hanging in the middle of the room. Any actual bright light will ruin the images as he's processing them. I'm in the dry room, with the wet room through another curtain. Ian had been so proud when he explained this entire setup to me and how not everyone has enough space to separate their equipment from their chemicals.

I'd just been proud of him for having what he wanted and for knowing what to do with it. Everything he does makes me proud. It's a strange feeling, the pride and love I feel for him, but I drink it up every day.

His photograph storage is right here, easy for me to flip through to try to find the pieces I want to frame for him. He'll be thrilled, I know he will. Anytime I've taken interest in his work before, he's been so excited.

However, even though I could easily flip through his photos right now, I'm drawn to the wet room. Curiosity gets the best of me, and I really want to see what he's been working on. Pushing aside another heavy curtain lets me enter the other half of the darkroom. This one doesn't fall back perfectly into place, but I barely notice.

I have no idea how long Ian will be gone, and I don't want him to catch me down here. It's not that he'd be mad, but then the surprise would be blown.

First I walk to the photos hanging over the chemical trough. There's Molly, her mouth curved into a soft smile in her sleep. There are ones of me cooking, the sun coming through the window and making it look like I have a halo.

Yeah, right. I can't help but laugh at that.

The red glow from the overhead bulb makes the entire space feel eerie. These photos are all too new, too fresh. I need something he won't miss. I'm about to return to the dry area of Ian's darkroom when I see a box tucked behind the curtain. It's set off to the side, almost hidden. If the curtain had fallen back in place where it was supposed to when I entered, I never would have seen it.

The box has a lid and the word *private* scrawled across the front of it.

What in the world would my husband want to keep private down here?

I feel drawn to it, like there's a thread wrapped around my torso, tugging me forward.

Only I realize too late it's not a thread. It's a noose, and it's wrapped around my neck. Without thinking through what I'm doing, I pull the box out of its hiding place and flip off the lid. The photographs in here are all dry, all obviously much older than the ones hanging on the line. I check the upper right corner of the photograph in the front for the date written on it.

There it is, in pencil, almost two years ago.

My hands start to shake as I grab the bundle of photographs and pull them out. I sit down on the floor and rest them in my lap.

My mouth falls open when I realize what I'm looking at. They're photographs of me, from different angles, all of them with me as the focal point. That in itself isn't strange; I know I was Ian's favorite subject before Molly came along.

I flip to the next photo. I have to know more.

"No." The word is a prayer, but I barely hear it. "Dear God, no." My hands tremble. Without meaning to, my fingers tighten on the photograph, and it bends, but I manage to keep from tearing it.

It's suddenly clear Ian found the missing camera.

I've never seen myself look like this. There's an expression on my face that terrifies me, a grim expression, my mouth tight, my eyes narrow. It's difficult for me to tear my gaze away from my face, but I do, and then I see what's in my hand.

A knife. *The knife.*

I'm covered in blood. It's not red, of course, that's not a color he can create down here. The photographs are all black and white, but I know what the dark on my hands and arms is. I know what I've been doing. *And now Ian does, too.*

What's worse — if the date on these is to be believed, he's known for a long time. And he's never said anything.

The next photograph turns my stomach. The red light casts a horrid color on the page. I'm turned towards Ian, who's still awake, his head lifted, tilted to the side, but the hood makes it impossible to tell who it is for sure.

But I know. And I'm sure my husband does, too.

The photos get worse. Ian, covered in blood. A close-up of my hand as I stab him. The knife sinking into his leg.

Vomit rises in my throat, and I turn, getting sick on the floor. Using the back of my hand to wipe my mouth, I look at the photographs again.

No. No, no, no.

Someone is screaming that word, and then I realize it's me, the sound of my voice so loud in the darkroom that it hurts my ears. I push up from where I'm sitting and turn to leave, but my foot slips in my vomit. When I hit the floor, my teeth rattle together so hard tears spring to my eyes.

The photos fall from my grip and scatter across the floor.

For a moment I sit there, my sins on full display across the darkroom like some perverted art gallery; then I stand back up and stumble backwards, to the stairs.

I rush into the kitchen, kick over my mug. Coffee spreads across the floor, but I barely notice it.

My phone. Where's my phone?

I remember seeing it in the living room, and I run in there, heedless of where I'm tracking. For a moment I think Ian must have taken my phone, must have hidden it from me, but it's right on top of the book I was reading, a stupid little novella about love at Christmas and second chances.

He's saved as speed dial number one. I stab the screen to call him. Hold it to my ear.

Tears stream down my cheeks. *What will I say to him if he picks up? How will I smooth this over?*

It rings uselessly in my ear. I hear Ian's voice telling me to leave a message and that he'll get back to me.

I hang up. Put the phone on the counter.

Pick it back up and try again.

This time, he answers. He sounds out of breath, and I close my eyes, wondering how far he and Molly have gotten on their walk. I wonder if he's decided to go to the police, if after all this time, he's had enough.

"Hey, Beth, you okay?"

I realize I have to respond, or he's going to worry. Swallowing hard, I plaster a smile to my face. That's one thing I know — that smiling when you're on the phone can trick the other person into thinking you're happy.

Really, though, I'm falling apart.

"Hey, yeah, I just realized I forgot to give Molly her little lovey. I didn't know if she was missing it." My heart hammers hard as I lie to my husband.

"Oh, I don't think she noticed. She's fine. Listen, I think I'm going to take her over to the park. There's supposed to be some painters there today, painting nature scenes. I thought I'd like to check it out, but it means I'll be gone longer than I thought."

"That sounds great." I clear my throat. "Anything I can do for you while you're gone?"

"Nope, I'm good."

He sounds normal. If I didn't know what he had in the darkroom, I'd think everything was fine.

"Okay." I exhale hard. "Great, well, I'll see you two when you get back."

"Yep. I'm looking forward to it. I love you, Beth. More than anything."

"More than anything."

I hang up. Put the phone down on the counter. Stare at it.

I'm standing still, but my mind races as I try to think through what just happened.

Ian knows.

Ian knows.

And he's known for a while.

And he still loves me.

But I don't know what to do with that information.

I want to call him again, ask him what he's doing with the photographs. I want to make him tell me he loves me, make him promise me he won't do anything with them.

I want to burn them.

But, if he's to be believed, he has copies of everything uploaded to the cloud. Even if I were to burn them, they're still there.

Oh, God.

I'm not sure what to do, but I know I have to move. I'll start by cleaning up my mess. The thought of my vomit on the floor, of his photographs scattered so he'll be sure to know I found them, spurs me on. I race to the pantry to get paper towels and cleaning supplies, then hurry back down the stairs.

He'll be gone for a while, but I don't have the luxury of

taking my time. It will smell in his darkroom, but the terrible smell of his chemicals will cover it up, I'm sure of that.

I'll just have to keep him out of here for a while until the smell is completely gone.

First, I pick up the scattered photographs. It's impossible for me to look at them, and I put them back in the box, moving faster now as I gain more confidence.

If Ian knows and never said anything, then there must be a reason why.

Does it matter the reason as long as he never tells anyone the truth?

How can I keep him from doing that?

I just have to keep him happy.

The thought hits me, and I pause. That's it. He's happy, and that's why he hasn't said anything about them. I don't want to lose Ian, don't want to lose Molly. I'll keep him happy.

I'll be the perfect wife.

I already know how.

THANK YOU FOR READING

Did you enjoy reading *You Can't Hide*? Please consider leaving a review on Amazon. Your review will help other readers to discover the novel.

ABOUT THE AUTHOR

Emily Shiner always dreamed of becoming an author but first served her time as a banker and a teacher. After a lifetime of devouring stacks of thrillers, she decided to try her hand at writing them herself. Now she gets to live out her dream of writing novels and sharing her stories with people around the world. She lives in the Appalachian Mountains and loves hiking with her husband, daughter, and their two dogs.

ALSO BY EMILY SHINER

Printed in Great Britain
by Amazon

22291861R00138

Blipp Digital
Luke Bolger
William Bonner
Bronwen Booth
Steven Bourne
Greg Boyd
Russell Bradshaw
Gary Branch
James Branch
David Brand
Jorge Brandao
Toby Bray
Doug Bredo
Patrick Brennan
Carmen Bridgman
Michael Brindle
Mark Broadhurst
Alexandra Broadrick
Jeff Brodzinski Jr.
Mark Brooks
Ken Brough
Emile Broussard, M.D.
Michael Brown
Nicholas Brown
Simon Brown
Laura Bruce
Hans Brucker
Andrew Buchanan
Paul Buitink
Anthony Bunge
Martin Burgess
Klas Buring
James Burke
Nick Burke
Nigel Burman
Russell Burns
Jackie Bussey
Nick Busvine
Kevin Butcher
Sohail Butt
Joseph Byrne
Graham Cadd
Sarah Caddy
David Callander
Terence Calvert
Dave Campbell
Xander Cansell

Simon Cantrell
Steve Carpenter
Jeffrey Gerard Carter
Ray Carter
Steve Carter
    Be-Printed.com
Brian Cartmell
Dave Cartwright
Piers Caswell
Simon Caufield
Thomas Caulfield
Edoardo Cavallo
Dominic Cave
Matthew Chaddock
Yves Chambaz
Julia Chamberlain
Michael
    Chamberlayne
John Chambers
Paul Champness
Mark Chaney
Neil Cheatle
Adrian Chittock
Jay Chmelauskas
Inam Chohan
Doris Chou
Terran Churcher
I Churchward
Christopher Clark
Pete Clark
Martin Clarke
Ross Clarke
Russell Clarke
Susan Clarke
Tony Clarke
Roger Clarnette
Chris Cleaver
James Clegg
Alan Clelland
Hugo Clugston
Jock Coats
Philip Cockayne
Patrick Coghill
Howard Cohen
Rob Coles
Stevyn Colgan
Charles Collett
Andrea Colombo

Killian Connolly
Peter Connon
Gavan Convery
David Cooke
John Cooksey
David Cookson
Burt Coons
Dominic Cooper
Paul Cooper
John Corbit
Brent Cornelius
Colin Corp
Elspeth Corrigan
Declan Cosgrove
    GoldMadeSimple.com
Michael Coulson
Krystyna Coupe
Gary Cowd
Barnaby Cox
Jason Cozens
Jason Cozens
Andrew Craig
Oldemiro Cravo
Steve Creasy
Charles Creswick
David Crevier
Aaron Crozier
Mark Crump
Alan Cunnane
John Cunnane
James Cunningham
Cathy Cuthbert
James Dakin
Damien Daly
James Daly
Howard Daniel
Trevor Daniels
Donald Darmanin
Geoffrey Darnton
Barrie Davey
Mike Davis
Tim Davis
Tracy Davis
Rupert Degas
Joe de Kadt
Gary Delaney
Koen De Mulder